I0691389

Exposed

First Edition

Published by the Nazca Plains Corporation
Las Vegas, Nevada
2014

ISBN: 978-1-61098-356-3
E-Book: 978-1-61098-357-0

Published by
The Nazca Plains Corporation®
Paradise Rd, Suite 141
Las Vegas, NV 89109-8000

PUBLISHER'S NOTE
Exposed is a work of fiction created wholly by Christopher Trevor's imagination. All characters are fictional and any resemblance to any persons living or deceased is purely by accident. No portion of this book reflects any real person or events.

Cover Photo, CURAphotography
Art Director, Blake Stephens

This book is dedicated to:

Dave and his Speedos, Willie and his red sweat socks, Eric, the mystery man on the train and his fetishy looking sandals, and as always, Timmy Backman, for unending inspiration.

Exposed

First Edition

Christopher Trevor

Contents

Dave, Taken by Surprise

I arrived at Dave's house an hour earlier than the time we had agreed upon. I love surprising the handsome mature well-built guy, and if I can have another chance at teasing and tormenting him erotically, well, you know that I'm going to go for it. Its how I roll after all, as the new saying seems to go.

It was a warm and sunny morning that day. Dave and I had agreed to meet for brunch that Wednesday at 12:30 PM, which would have given Dave more than enough time for his hour and a half to two hour morning workout at the gym and then a couple of hours of sleep when he got back home. Dave said that sleeping a bit to relax the body after a workout of lifting weights and aerobics was very healthy… and it was those couple of hours of sleep that Dave treated himself to after his workout that I was counting on that morning.

Using the key that Dave had given me I quietly let myself into his house. Closing the door behind me and locking it I called out, "Dave, are you here buddy?" not all that loudly, but still loud enough so he would hear me letting myself in. I didn't want to alarm the handsome guy after all, just have some mean kinky fun with him. It was after we had become really good sex buddies that Dave had granted me the key to his house, in a way I felt as if the handsome guy had granted me the key to his kingdom, he himself being the kingdom that is, my sexy kingdom.

Not many people would understand my relationship with Dave, in the way that I enjoy having sex with him, mixing it up with tenderness and loving yet with some nastiness thrown in as well. But when Dave submitted to me and decided to trust me in that I would at times torment the hell out of him but never do him any permanent harm, well, suffice to say, a very special friendship was born. And since then I treasure every moment with Dave, even the moments he's not expecting, like the one I'm telling you about herein.

When Dave did not respond to my calling out his name I put his house key back in my backpack and made my way slowly up the stairs toward his bedroom. If I played my cards right Dave and I would be having dinner instead of brunch. A sort of evil grin played over my lips as I quietly ascended the stairs.

When I reached the top of the stairs I looked down the short hallway toward Dave's bedroom. The door was halfway open and I was treated to the sight of a pair of white sweat socked feet at the foot of Dave's queen sized bed.

Perfect! Dave had been to the gym for his early morning workout and was now taking a power-nap, as he called it, before our brunch date…

I walked very softly down the short hallway, past the bathroom. I pushed the bedroom door open the rest of the way and quietly gasped, breathed in, and marveled at the sight of Dave as he lay sleeping peacefully on his bed, outside the covers. On the floor beside his bed I saw a pair of Nike sneakers, Dave's gym shorts and his tee shirt. His sounds of breathing were gentle and calming and he was truly beautiful lying there in just a red and white Speedo and a pair of calf-length white sweat socks. Obviously Dave had again fulfilled his erotic fetish of wearing a Speedo rather than traditional underwear when he had worked out that morning at the gym.

The way some men I know, including myself, who have a fetish for men's black socks, men's feet, spanking, bondage and other erotic leanings, Dave has a fetish for wearing Speedos or thongs or very skimpy sexy underpants under his clothing. And on that day he had obviously worn his red and white Speedo under his gym gear for his workout. I knew he hadn't showered yet and I also knew that that silk Speedo would smell "and taste" heavenly when I got my nose, mouth and tongue on it. But first other things had to be tended to.

Dave was like a male Sleeping Beauty as he lay there in his near nakedness. I was counting on his being a deep sleeper to help me to accomplish what I had in mind for my handsome Canadian prince on this day…

I slowly and silently approached the bed, quietly unzipping my backpack as I went…

When Dave and I first met online he did not allude to being kinky at all, except for his fetish for wearing Speedos, and that was mostly what drew me to him. When I saw the pictures of him that he sent me of him clad in just a Speedo, a thong or some other form of sexy underwear I have to say that he took my breath away. I knew that somehow I would have to be able to seduce this mature handsome guy to my wiles... he was that delicious and appetizing looking, just the kind of guy that I would love to torment and devour over and over... and devouring him is just SO very much fun...

It was during one of our first online sex sessions as we came to call them that I introduced Dave to the joys of being blindfolded while being teased and literally devoured in a sexual sense. During that first romp I had told Dave that I would take the blindfold off him if he was feeling any kind of fear. I kissed and nuzzled his lips, neck and ears as I spoke to him about the blindfold he was currently wearing.

"Oh God Chris, you're loving me in ways I've never known before," Dave blurted as he gently pushed my hand away from the knot in his blindfold that was tied behind his head. "Leave the blindfold on me, I am a bit afraid but I somehow trust you at the same time."

The way he said that he was a bit afraid about being blindfolded touched my heart and I ached for the guy all the more. I held him tight and sucked one of his earlobes, licking the cloth of the blindfold at the same time, assuring him that I would NEVER hurt him, just tease and torment him in a sexual fashion.

And so it went that with our next sex sessions Dave simply took it for granted that he would be blindfolded... and always in his Speedo or a pair of ultra sexy underpants to spur me on to devour him all the more.

Dave came to realize how I loved teasing him, tormenting him, driving him over the edge of sexual frenzy, but at the same time loving me for it. He had submitted to me in erotic trust and each time we met I adored him all the more for it.

As I thought these things I slowly brought out of my backpack what I would need as I approached my sleeping prince...

When I first met Dave it was in an online chat room and admittedly it was his screen name with the word Speedos in it that caused me to IM him first, saying hello politely to see if he would be willing to chat with me for a bit. I was very elated to find that he was willing to chat with me and a few minutes later we exchanged pictures of each other. I always enjoy knowing what the person I am talking to looks like when chatting online and I like for them to know what I look like as well. A lot of guys, for whatever the reason do not like sending out their picture, they see someone asking them for a picture of themselves as perhaps being judgmental or stalker-like, for me though it's simply a matter of putting a face to the person I am presently chatting with.

When I saw Dave's picture my heart felt like it had jumped into my mouth because the older mature handsome guy reminded me of another older mature man, one that I used to see on the subway once in a while on my way to work in the mornings when I would make a connection to a local train. Whenever I would see the older man on the train I was drawn to him because he was always dressed in a very dapper manner... old fashioned sports jackets, loafers with awesome looking silk dress socks, a necktie tied nice and tight at his collar, and at times an old fashioned cap on his head. The older man used to be sitting with his eyes closed while riding the train and for whatever the reason he always had a look as if he were in pain somehow. I remember watching as he would sit clenching and unclenching his hands sometimes, for whatever the reason. While looking at him one morning when he was dressed in a pink dress shirt with a beige sports jacket, brown slacks, brown silk socks and brown loafers I suddenly had a vision of him naked except for his white briefs, which given his age I guessed would have been "Fruit of the Loom" briefs. As I allowed the fantasy to go through my mind I saw the older man in just his briefs with his hands tied behind him, blindfolded and being led down a long flight of stairs to a basement of some sort... and the older man saying to the person holding him by the arms from behind, "I don't know why you're doing this to me." I never went any further with that fantasy, and I had never found myself attracted to an older man before or after that, until I met Dave in the online chat room. I hadn't even thought about the older man on the train in a long while, as I hadn't seen him anymore once my hours at work were changed and I no longer took the train I would see him on. I often wondered just who he was, where he was headed each day... but most of all I wondered what kind of room it was that he was being led down to in my fantasy. In a way Dave helped to answer that last question. It would be a room where he would be sexually teased, tormented, a room that he would dread being brought to yet loved being forced into each time he was taken there.

So when Dave and I exchanged pictures I told him how he reminded me of the older man on the train and how I pictured him blindfolded in my fantasy, I hadn't yet told Dave of my fetish for bondage as well. I wanted to move slowly because I got the feeling that Dave and I could be long term friends... and I didn't want to scare him away... I did want to scare him a bit though... LOL... just to tease him...

We began our chat that day like any other. When I saw Dave on my buddy list I typed "Hey there Dave how's my Speedo buddy?" and pressed "Send."

"I am doing great today," Dave responded. "How about you?"

"Doing great as well," I typed, already feeling the tingling in my cock as I chatted with my Speedo buddy. "I am so glad you liked the sound of my erotic fantasy that I told you about yesterday. I remember one of the first times I saw that well dressed older man. I pictured myself holding him by his upper arms, him blindfolded, wearing just his briefs and leading him down a flight of stairs into a bedroom/ playroom of some sort. He looked sort of the submissive type to me I suppose."

"Yes, it sounds very interesting," Dave said.

"I admit, it was a strange fantasy, even for me," I said next, and then next planting the seed which I hoped would take fruition. "Dave, could you see yourself in that position with me, perhaps wearing nothing more than a tight white Speedo?"

"Well, I've got a couple of white Speedos," Dave responded as my heart thundered. "You would have to be the judge as to how tight they are on me."

"Well, with my fetish for black dress socks I could easily see you in a tight white Speedo, a pair of knee length black silk socks and a blindfold tied over your eyes as I tease you," I said, plunging in.

"MMMMMM and I think I could go along with that," Dave replied. "I always dressed for the office when I worked in a suit and tie… always wore white underwear and black knee length silk socks."

"Your socks that you would be wearing in the fantasy would be leftover from the workday," I suggested.

"Yes, I used to wear knee high socks and I've always liked white bikini underpants," Dave said. "I even have a few thongs."

"Nice, real nice," I said. "I think what makes my scene idea fun is that being that the older sexy guy is blindfolded he is wondering just what this younger guy has in mind for him."

"Oh yes, I'm sure that would be a wonder for the older man," Dave said. "And hopefully nothing would be too outrageous that is in store for him... *or me*, if you prefer."

"Of course not," I typed quickly, wanting to reassure Dave. "But I would enjoy your feeling of anticipation as I lead you along carefully, teasing you a bit by kissing and nipping the back of your neck, such a sensitive spot for so many guys. I would also tease you perhaps by squeezing your ass in your Speedos, tease you verbally a bit as well, and just to keep you wondering what all I have planned for you."

"MMMMMM, thinking I would like that," Dave said. "Especially the kissing part... and oh yes, the feeling of my ass being squeezed turns me on and makes me horny."

I smiled and typed, whispering in your ear, "Are you regretting this at all? Handing yourself over to me?" as I tug at the knot in your blindfold. I step in front of you and tweak and kiss your jutted up nipples a few times as well.

"OH MY GOD," Dave responded. "You've really got me now. I would let you take me anywhere and do almost anything to me... as long as you kiss and bight my nips... driving me crazy."

"Being blindfolded makes this all the more intense doesn't it Dave?" I asked the guy as I circled him, adoring the sight of him before me, trailing my fingertips against his Speedo covered testicles, squeezing them a bit as I kissed his tits again and again.

As I squeezed his tits hard the guy hoisted himself to his tiptoes and he heard me whisper, "Thank you for trusting me to do this to you."

"And thank you for taking the time to adore me in such a way," Dave said back to me. "I want you to do with me as you like... this is an amazing feeling."

"You may regret that at some point," I whispered in Dave's ear, making him shudder a bit as I sucked at his earlobe.

Dave realized I was playing head games, but at the same time he could not tear himself away.

"Standing behind you," I typed. "Holding your arms tight near the shoulders you feel my hard cock in my pants as it presses against your Speedo covered ass, my lips right by your ear."

"OH, loving the way you are nibbling on my ears," Dave said and I could almost hear his heavy breathing. "And feeling up my balls through my tight Speedo... if you look down you will see a wet patch as pre cum starts to flow."

"Your hands are not tied Dave," I said teasingly. "Why don't you just take off the blindfold? Or is it more exciting this way?"

Dave's breath did indeed come in gasps and yes, I did see the pre cum staining the front of his Speedo. I grinned at the sight of it... and knelt down in front of him.

"I lick your erection through your Speedo as my hands are palmed and running up and down your silk socked calves," I typed. "And you won't take the blindfold off because you know that it keeps all of this a mystery for you, am I right?"

"I don't want to spoil the moment by taking off the blindfold," Dave said. "I find that I like the idea of not knowing what and where you are going to touch me nowwwww…"

Dave howled as my tongue snaked down to his balls in his Speedo.

"Don't lose your balance now handsome fella," I teased and snapped the elastic in Dave's socks against his calves. "You really have no idea where I might have positioned you. I kissed the bulge in his Speedos, the taste and smell was electric."

"I am sure you would have me by your bed so if I fall I will be in a position wherein you can take advantage of me," Dave typed as a suggestion.

"Do you like to cum in your Speedo Dave?" I asked. "Is that part of the thrill for you when it comes to wearing them?"

As I spoke I hauled the guy back to his feet.

"OH yesssssss, loving the kiss on my cock through my Speedo," Dave replied.

"Unknown to you I have a glass with ice cubes in it nearby," I typed. "I squeeze the back of your neck and hug you against me for a moment. You make the perfect guy for me to play these games with Dave. Then, I pop an ice cube between my teeth and press it against your naked back. I slowly trail the ice cube up and down your back with my mouth. You let out a loud sexy grunting sound."

"I whisper back to you that so far I like what you have been doing to me," Dave said. "Pressing myself against you..."

"You shivering as the ice cube sends chills through you," I said next.

"Yes, I am shivering as you run the ice cube up and down my back, I cry out with joy," Dave responded happily.

"I squat down at your ass cheeks and allow the ice cube to fall into the space between your Speedo and your ass," I said teasingly. "You wiggle around so sexily. I reach into your Speedo with two hands, cup your delectable ass cheeks in my hands, and squeeze them. I whisper in your ear, "Squeeze your own tits this time Dave. As I squeeze your ass cheeks you move so sexy...""

"Feeling the ice cube slide down my ass crack as you push it in my Speedo," Dave said. "Wiggling my ass, trying to get it to slide further down, and then I do as you say and pinch my tits, making them hard and swollen... wanting to do this to yours as well."

"Oh I know you do," I responded, sounding as sexy harsh as possible. "I know you want to do that to my tits, now you just have to figure out why I blindfolded you for this. I'm going to go so slow Dave, I know how to play you now... and I plan to play you like a musical instrument... I sidle up behind you and hold you oh so close to me again. You gave away a secret Dave, keep twisting your tits, do as I say; it drives me nuts to have you in this way. I am now running my hands slowly down your arms, because now I'm going to make you jump right out of those long socks.... Your mouth drops open as you wonder what I plan to do to you next..."

"Oh yes please, do you want me naked in front of you?" Dave asked.

"I lower your Speedo in back, exposing your well-shaped ass cheeks," I said as I slowly rolled Dave's Speedo down in back. "I gasp at the sight of them as I kneel behind you and teasingly say, "Stay balanced now Dave." I give your ass cheeks a few wet slurpy kisses as I grip them and part them, exposing your pink hole. It seems to twitch and gape as I spit in it a few times. You look upwards in blindfolded darkness, grunting and swearing. I then tell you to let go of your tits."

"MMMMM, feeling your hands gripping my ass cheeks now and your hot kisses..." Dave typed quickly. "Feeling your spit on my hole running down as I feel your finger rub it in."

"Then, my tongue invaded your most private crevice," I said.

"Doing as I am told, I let my hands fall to my sides," Dave said.

"Yes, your hands shaking then as I tongue your hole," I said to Dave. "The sounds of slurping and sucking drives you crazy, the feel of my tongue inside you makes you break out in goose bumps."

"I reach around now to help spread my ass cheeks so that you can get your tongue deep inside me," Dave said.

"Good boy," I replied.

"My body is trembling as you push your tongue at my hole and me feeling your tongue entering me," Dave said.

"Am I making you crazy Dave?" I asked. "Is your head spinning? I flip my tongue greedily against your ass walls."

"Yes, you are driving me crazy for sure," Dave agreed. "I love all that you are doing to me, making me want to feel more of you in me."

I laughed and said, "We will get there buddy, but for now I'm going to feast on this pucker hole of yours for a while more."

"I trail a hand down your sexy legs and socked calves as you hold your ass cheeks spread for me," I typed.

"Me bending forward a bit to let you have better access to my hole," Dave said. "I cry out with pleasure as your tongue works over my hot asshole."

"I sit down on the bed that I have you standing near," I typed. "I want you in a prone position as I eat your hole more and more. A few moments later you are in position on my lap with your legs wrapped around my upper body and your asshole in my face."

"Oh man, look at these mounds," I whisper and gently bight your ass cheeks."

"Alright Christopher, you helped me get there and into this position so I will be glad to have you eat out my ass all night long," Dave said in passion. "OHHHHHHHHHH YESSSSSS..."

"I get you into position, loving every moment of you allowing me to control you," I said. "Whispering thank you in between bighting your ass cheeks and then spreading them open yet again. I grin as I pick up a bottle of heated strawberry edible lube."

"Now Dave, get ready for the opposite of the ice cube," I said, sounding villainous as I began slathering Dave's hole with the lube, squirting a few drops of it into his hole at the same time."

The lube instantly began to warm up as it touched the walls of Dave's hole…

"OOOOOOOHHH MYYYYYY GODDDDD," Dave cried out. "OH YES, I love the feel of whatever you just put on me…"

Then, I began licking and sucking the warm liquid from Dave's hole…

"I'm eventually going to fuck you like nobody's business Dave," I said in a threatening manner.

Dave wiggled his ass against my face; he loved the tonguing I was giving him…

"But before I do fuck you I'm going to plug your hole with a butt-plug and tongue your balls for a while," I said. "You won't cum buddy… not till I say so…"

"Oh yes…" Dave whispered in response to me. "I want to have you fuck me over and over again."

I smiled and said, "It's going to be a long night."

"Oh, I am hoping for a long night," Dave said. "I truly like all that you have put me through so far… and I know that it can only get better with you in control."

"Or worse Dave," I teased my Speedo buddy.

Then, I began to slowly insert a pink latex thick butt-plug into Dave's hole, wiggling it in slowly, so slowly. Dave hunched himself up a bit so that his ass was now high in the air.

"OHHHHH, I'm sure you would not harm me in any way…"Dave murmured after my comment about making things worse for him. "You really are too nice of a guy…"

But then, a new sound escaped Dave as he moaned, "OOOOOOO GOD," as the butt-plug entered him.

"Ohhhhhhhhhh, I have never had a butt-plug in me before…" Dave swooned.

I chuckled a tad meanly at his response and said, "No Dave, I would not harm you, there's too much more that I want to put you through, I want you to trust me... but I want to play my games as well."

"You are being so kind by slowly inserting it," Dave whispered.

Once the plug was in I gave Dave's socked feet and calves a few licks. I loved the taste of his manly feet.

"Mmmmmmmmmmmmmm feels niceeeeeeee," Dave squeaked as I licked his feet and the butt-plug filled his back door.

Dave now found himself balanced up on his open palmed hands and in a prone position in front of me as I nibbled at the bottoms of his socked feet.

"God, I've got a handsome older guy in a Speedo and black socks totally in my control," I whispered.

"Glad I'm not ticklish," Dave chuckled.

I pressed Dave's feet against my face and kissed them hard...

The plug in his hole felt like immense pressure after a while... but pleasurable at the same time...

"Only half in a Speedo as I can feel the air on my bare ass..." Dave said back. "But not a problem... It actually feels like I have a cock wedged in there but not all the way... OH GOD, I love that you thought of this, I'll plan to have it done more often to me..."

"On your feet!" I ordered then.

Being blindfolded and climbing to his feet with a butt-plug in his hole was not easy for the Speedo guy, but I sure did admire his persistence. When he was finally standing I grabbed the base of the butt-plug and inserted it the rest of the way.

"Standing up as fast as I can," Dave typed. "But staggering a bit as I go…"

"OOOOOOOOO…" Dave suddenly moaned as the butt-plug hit home inside him.

"Ohhhhhhhhhhh," Dave said then. "OH YESSSSSSS, that feels greatttttt…"

"You then feel me wrapping two straps around your waist that are attached to the plug," I typed. "This will insure that it stays wedged in you buddy."

Once the butt-plug was secured inside Dave I kissed his lips numerous times as I pushed the butt-plug in some more… and Dave moaned and kissed me back. As I kissed him I secured the straps around his waist, just above his sexy white Speedo. As I did my work Dave greedily kissed me and kissed me. He sucked my tongue as I slipped it into his mouth.

"Do you trust me now Dave?" I asked him, my lips then pressed against his blindfolded eyes, kissing them gently.

"Yes Christopher, I trust you," Dave responded as I kissed his blindfolded eyes.

"Then don't move," I said next and stepped away from him, grinning meanly.

As Dave stood there in blindfolded darkness, wearing just a Speedo, knee high black socks and with a butt-plug wedged tightly into his hole and said butt-plug strapped into his hole via the straps buckled around his waist I picked up a remote control device. With that mean looking grin on my face I clicked the "ON" button on the remote control… and the butt-plug wedged inside my Speedo guy began vibrating.

"Wondering what you have in mind for me," Dave typed next. "And knowing that whatever it is will be for your pleasure... and mine..."

Suddenly, Dave was engulfed in goose bumps...

"By now you would want to cum like crazy," I typed to my butt-plugged blindfolded buddy. "But my game is to edge my Speedo and socks guy for as long as possible, all night I hope..."

I kissed Dave again on the lips as he felt the butt-plug vibrating wildly deep inside him.

"Oh yes, my whole body has goose bumps," Dave said breathlessly and reached out to hold tightly to my shoulders, groping in his blindfolded darkness, not wanting to fall over. "I'm being overwhelmed and devoured with the sheer pleasure you are giving me."

I loved it as he held onto me...

"Oh Dave, what a find you are..." I said breathlessly and led the guy over to a wall.

I leaned him against the wall and ordered him not to move, and then he felt me slowly pulling his white Speedo down in front. Dave reached out and hugged me oh so close to him.

"Oh Christopher, feeling your hot body makes things get even better between us," Dave typed. "AND OH GOD, I feel the vibrator tormenting my hot tunnel, its sending sheets upon sheets of joy through me..."

Dave's cock pointed straight up at the ceiling and his balls hung nice and low, as big as two kiwis in his sexy sac... I strummed my fingertips lightly over the Speedos guy's dangling testicles...

"Oh yes, I feel your fingers playing with my balls now, like you said, playing me like I was a musical instrument," Dave hemmed breathlessly. "I love what you have created here Christopher…"

"Oh God Dave, I meant it when I said you were a good find…" I whispered as I stood next to him and fingered and rolled his balls in my hand.

He pressed himself harder up against the wall and gasped loudly…

"Christopher," Dave whispered huskily. "You are one very sexy guy… and I like what you have got me into here…"

I quickly typed, "If we could do this for real I would drive you crazy for sure… I'm really glad you like it, play my games Dave, play all my games please, I promise you a great time every time…

Then, Dave arched his head back and hoisted himself a bit to his tiptoes as I began slathering my tongue over his sweaty balls. I could feel his balls vibrating a bit to the butt-plug that was wedged deep inside him…

"OHHHHHHHHHHH… OH YES, lick my balls Christopher, I love that, and I love that… and I love that, I REALLY LOVE THAT," my Speedo guy grunted breathlessly, sounding as if he was just about crying behind his blindfold. "You said that I was a great find, so are you buddy, SO ARE YOU."

I held tight to Dave's sexy thighs, gripping them hard as he danced real sexily on his toes as I licked his balls like they were ice cream. His hard cock dribbled massive sized droplets of pre seed and it snaked down the sides of his throbbing shaft as his slit stared up at the ceiling. Dave pressed the palms of his hands against the wall I had him leaning against and by then he was crying tears of joy as I licked his balls a few more times, and then, then… began snaking the tip of my tongue up and along the outside of his cock shaft, the most sensitive part of a guy's erection.

As I licked and even planted kisses on Dave's erection I slid his Speedo down, down, down his legs, stripping him of it, leaving him in just his tall black silk socks, a blindfold tied over his eyes, and the butt-plug playing a song called "Vibrate in his pucker hole." As Dave stood now with his prized Speedo puddled around his socked feet I teased and tormented him anew by licking and kissing the underside of his erect cock.

"OHHHHHHHH... OH GOD, I feel it Christopher, my balls are really cooking up a big load here, and I need to cum buddy... I really need to cum..." Dave swooned through clenched teeth.

Looking up at him I felt my own cock tingling in my pants. I was hard as steel just watching as he pleaded about his need to shoot his load... to cum...

A few seconds later I was standing next to Dave, no longer teasing his cock by licking it, instead as he stood there practically at attention now with his hands behind his back he shuddered and writhed as I ran the pad of my tongue slowly around and around the tip of his pre seed oozing slit... Standing there Dave breathed heavily and from deep down in his chest. I loved watching his muscular hairy chest expand up and down and in and out as he reacted to my gentle rolling touch on his cock tip.

"Need to cum, want to cum, GOD, you're edging me here Christopher..." Dave whispered and even though his hands were not properly bound behind him he made no move near his throbbing cock.

The butt-plug in his hole cooked his ass walls and caused him to dance real sexily in his socks as it went on tormenting him back there...

What I had in mind at that point was fiendish as all hell but I knew that Dave could take it... I had faith in him after all...

<BIG EVIL GRIN>

"I do hope you're ready for what's coming next Dave," I typed and suddenly grabbed the guy's erection in my fist, squeezing it a bit. "Because what's coming next... is you bud..."

As I spoke I gave Dave's throbbing erect cock a few pulls and tugs, and that was all it took... the guy gushed a load that was big and potent enough to choke a goat.

"OOOHHHHHHHHHHH....OH   MY...   OH FUCK..." Dave grunted throatily as I held his spurting cock tight and his load sluiced all over his chest, nipples and stomach regions. "OHHHHHHHHH MY LORD... I'M CUMMING... am I ever cumming, oh Christopher... my Christopher..."

But then, as Dave shot his load, the tingling and buzzing sensations in his pucker hole from the vibrating butt-plug seemed to intensify.

"OOOOOOOOOOOO... wh-what's happening here???" Dave suddenly blurted in a mixture of the forced ecstasy and the sudden feeling of erotic pain in his hole.

"I guess you didn't know Dave, that if a guy shoots his load while something big is wedged up inside his hole that the pain from the device in there increases about a hundred and ten percent," I chuckled meanly and the guy danced as I tugged his cock some more.

Unbelievably he shot more and more thick ropes of creamy jazz, some of it even landed on his lips and he licked it and swallowed it down.

"OHHHHHHHHHH this is awesome, it feels so good yet it hurts so much at the same time Christopher... oooooooooo my poor pucker hole..." Dave seethed.

Finally, when Dave was done spurting his load all over himself I whipped the blindfold off him and whirled him around facing away from me...

As he stood there panting and grunting in a man's passion I undid the straps on the butt-plug and slowly and methodically wedged it out of his pucker hole...

"AWWWWWWW..." Dave roared then, his hole feeling super sensitive as I slowly inched the buzzing device out of him... and then meanly slid it back in.

"OH my fucks," Dave crooned and leaned forward, pressing one hand HARD against the wall and grabbing his cock with his other hand...

I was totally in awe, watching as I teased my Speedo guy with the butt-plug, fucking him in and out with it as he again stroked his cock. In what seemed like no time Dave was hard and at full mast... AGAIN...

"Oh my God," I whispered, watching as Dave stroked his hard cock like a madman, driving himself crazy it seemed as I did the deed of driving him crazy as well.

"OH YES, yes, fuck my pucker hole," Dave begged and the shot his load a second time, all over the wall in front of him.

I jammed the butt-plug deep inside him one last time and he spurted and spewed more the second time than he had the first time. A feeling beyond amazement and total ecstasy engulfed me, as I knew at that moment that I had a true treasure in this man named Dave who had a fetish for wearing a Speedo while in my clutches.

"AWWWWWW, enough now Chris, ENOUGH," Dave panted and I gently pulled the vibrating but-plug from his pucker hole.

"OH MY WORD," Dave thundered throatily, turned around facing me and pulled me into his arms, holding me close and tight, kissing my neck, my shoulders, my earlobes and my face and mouth. "You've opened up a whole new world for me Chris, a whole new way of making love... OH MY WORD..."

As this older mature and in such great shape man held me and kissed me and hugged me my own cock grew hard between my legs and Dave did not hesitate for a moment. He slowly slid to his knees in front of me, kneeling on his discarded Speedo and slurped my manhood into his velvet-like mouth, caressing it with his lips at the same time...

Feeling my cock grow hard and rigid now in present time I quickly stopped thinking about the past and concentrated on the present, at the moment at hand, at Dave sleeping after his workout, enjoying his power-nap, looking like a TRUE male sleeping beauty, and wearing just his red and white Speedo and white calf-length sweat socks. Smiling at my handiwork, at the fact that I now had Dave right where I wanted him I joined my handsome Canadian prince on the bed. I began by gently spreading his legs apart a bit and scurrying my way between them, to paradise, to the area of Dave's crotch that I adore and could feast on for hours on end...

I gently grabbed Dave's thighs and pressed my face against his Speedo covered crotch area...

"Mmmmm..." Dave crooned in his sleepy state.

I began licking and slurping at his Speedo, sniffing deeply and inhaling his manly scent of sweat and spunk from his earlier work out. It was a scent born of true man, true musculature and it was the scent of a man who had very recently worked out real hard. Oh yes, my Canadian prince was pumped up and ready for what I had in mind for him, the only thing was, he wasn't aware of it yet. As I thought that I grinned devilishly and nuzzled my nose and mouth harder against his Speedo covered crotch area.

"Oh Dave," I whispered, loving the feel of the silk material of his Speedo against my face, and loving the feel of what was inside that Speedo against my face as well.

At the sound of my voice and the feel of my face on his Speedo Dave slowly opened his eyes and whispered my name, "C-Chris?"

"Yes my Canadian prince, don't get scared, it's just me…" I said softly, but not whispering now.

Once more I licked and kissed Dave's crotch area, pressing my face against his Speedo and again inhaled his glorious male scent.

"MMMM, that feels wonderful," Dave grunted, cleared his throat of the sleep and lifted his legs a bit as I caressed his thighs a bit, squeezing them.

"OHHHHH yes, wonderful way to wake up from my power nap Chris," Dave said lovingly, slowly opening his beautiful eyes. "Just can't believe you didn't sneak a blindfold on me while I was aslee – OH HOLY SHIT!!!"

Looking up and as he tried to move his hands to run his fingers through my hair poor Dave in his Speedo and sweat socks realized with a mixture of dismay and excitement…

"I-I'm tied at my wrists to the bed board here!" Dave exclaimed, tugging at the ropes that I had used to secure him to his bed board, his wrists tied in a crisscross fashion. "Oh my word, my USA stud, however did you manage this???"

"Let's just say I'm glad you're a sound sleeper my Canadian prince," I replied with a grin on my face, leaning down and smooching Dave's crotch area a few times, getting some grunts and groans of a man's passion out of him and then looking back up at him as he squirmed in his bonds. "I honestly cannot believe that you slept through it as I raised your wrists up to that bed board and then tied them to it buddy. I was thinking that you were maybe playing possum and were simply once again allowing me my fun."

As I spoke I snapped the elastic waistband in Dave's Speedo against his skin and watched in wonderment as he tried in vain to get his wrists untied.

"Trust me on this BUD, I was fast asleep, no sleeping guy would allow himself to be bound up like this," Dave said to me, sounding exasperated but at the same time the erection that had sprung up in his Speedo was testament to the fact that he was indeed aroused by his latest predicament. "Okay Chris, you've got me, obviously. But now that you've got me this way, what all do you plan to do with me???"

"As if you didn't know my Canadian prince," I replied breathlessly and reached again into my backpack, and brought out more rope.

"Oh my word, I have a feeling I may want to be blindfolded for whatever you're planning this time..." Dave panted as I stood up, grabbed one of his white sweat socked feet by the ankle and hoisted it up and bent it back as far as possible toward the bed board. "OH FUCK..."

As I twined rope around and around Dave's socked ankle I sniffed and snuffed at his foot... Like his Speedo Dave's sweat socks smelled of a man who had very recently worked out real hard, real fucking hard...

The way the muscles in Dave's biceps and triceps flexed every time he tried to untie his hands proved just how hard this older mature man worked out... and I for one am ecstatic over the shape he keeps himself in, so well-muscled, so well-toned, so beautiful...

A short while later Dave was in a semi-bent "U" shaped position with his wrists and now his bent back legs tied to his bed board.

"OH my word, what a position I'm in here," Dave ranted, wiggling his socked feet as the bottoms of them looked up at the ceiling.

"Feeling scared this time Dave?" I teased him meanly as I again reached into my backpack.

"I-I-do I have reason to be?" Dave asked. "You told me that if I allowed you to do these things to me that you would never hurt me Chris. I'm praying now that that hasn't changed."

The way he sounded like he was pleading was music to my ears and heart. And the look of desperation in his beautiful eyes broke my heart and made me fall in love with him all the more... it was that look of desperation that I craved from him, that feeling of being unsure about me at times that emanated from him.

"So glad I did a lot of stretching exercises after I worked out earlier," Dave said, looking up at the ceiling as he spoke. "This sure is a hell of a position to twist a poor unsuspecting guy into... and... oh my word..."

Dave cut himself off in mid-sentence when he saw that what I had taken out of my backpack next was a sharp small pair of snipping scissors.

"What, what all do you plan to do with that Chris?" Dave asked, real fear showing in his eyes at that point. "Please man…"

"Before I answer your question Dave, I'll need you to answer one for me," I replied, holding up the scissors and tweaking them in a cutting motion, opening and closing them.

"Sure, sure, what do you want to know bud?" Dave asked him also breathless at that moment.

"That Speedo that you're presently wearing, do you have another one just like it?" I asked him and with that question Dave did not need three guesses to know what I planned to do next.

"Yes, yes, you know I always buy at least three or four pairs of identical Speedos, especially if I like the style, the way I wear them all the time they wear out really fast and…" Dave replied and I made a cutting motion with the scissors, signaling him that he had said enough.

Then, to Dave's dismay I situated myself on the bed behind his raised buttocks area, opened the scissors to a cutting position and began by puncturing a tiny hole in Dave's silk Speedo, right against his ass crack…

"OH GOD, be careful Chris, PLEASE, be careful," Dave begged.

"Now Dave, my Canadian prince, would I hurt you bud?" I asked him and began cutting away his Speedo, beginning at the area of his ass crack.

"Y-you always said you would never hurt me man, and I'm holding you to that at this moment," Dave panted, tears in his eyes as I slowly cut away his Speedo, slowly revealing his ass crack that I adore.

"Wrong Dave, you are not holding me at the moment, I'm holding you bud," I replied fiendishly.

When the scissors reached the area where Dave's balls were he held his breath as I cut some more, trailing the side of the scissors against his testicles.

"Oh please Chris, my USA stud, please be careful," Dave whispered.

"I have to say Dave you're doing very well here today, I didn't even have to tell you not to move while I'm doing this," I teased him meanly.

"I-I didn't need to be told," Dave responded sheepishly as I was now leaning over him, looking down into his fear-filled eyes as I snipped and snipped at his ill-fated Speedo.

Finally, when I had literally cut the Speedo in two, right down the middle I put the scissors down on Dave's night table. I proceeded to yank the Speedo off him, it coming off in tatters in sections.

As I took Dave's Speedo off him, revealing the sweet spots of his that I adored the most Dave was panting and literally crying in relief. And I swear, his asshole was panting, gaping, breathing almost, dying for the attention Dave knew I was going to bestow upon it.

"Th-thank you Chris, thank you for not cutting me," Dave whispered as his tears flowed freely down his beautifully handsome face.

Once his Speedo was completely off him I tossed it aside and leaned down over his face. I kissed and licked Dave's tears away, kissed his eyes as well, and gently massaged his forehead a bit.

"You knew in your heart that I would not have harmed you Dave," I said and kissed his quivering lips. "But I am glad that I had you going for a while... just look how fear hard that cock of yours is now..."

"Oh yeah, sure," Dave replied sarcastically. "Being tied up while he's sleeping and then having his Speedo chopped off him with a razor sharp scissor will do that to most guys, make them fear hard that is..."

I chuckled a bit meanly, kissed Dave again on his lips and then scurried back to the prized area of my Canadian prince that I so thoroughly coveted.

Scant seconds later the sounds of Dave groaning and grunting in a man's heated passion filled the room, as I had laid down half off and half on my Canadian prince's bed, with my face planted directly at his gaping and wide open asshole...

Dave moaned crazily as I slithered my tongue inside him, devouring him back there, licking his ass walls, sucking at them, spitting inside him as deep as possible and gripping his upturned ass cheeks hard while I sucked my saliva greedily back out of his sopping wet asshole.

"AWWWWWWW, oh my word, this is amazing," Dave hawed, barely able to catch one even breath as I serviced his rear door area.

"Glad now that I tied you up while you were sleeping my Canadian prince?" I asked Dave before burying my face again in his hole and slithering and flicking my tongue around in there hungrily, like a dog in heat.

"OH YES, yes my USA stud, you can tie me up anytime you want, anytime at all," Dave panted. "Such things you do to me Christopher... never knew these games of yours could be so titillating... AWWWWWWW..."

Dave curled his toes back under his sweat socks and clenched his fingers into and out of fists as I ate his hole like it was to be my last meal... Dave's hole tasted from sweat, workout and silk from the Speedo he had been wearing while he had sweated and tortured himself earlier at the gym. But now it was my turn to torture him. As I again slithered my tongue inside his most private crevice, which was not all that private at the moment I licked the walls of Dave's hole and pre cum slithered like crazy from the wide sexy slit of his hard cock. His balls churned, cooking up a load of Canadian slime that was just itching to burst from his throbbing cock. Smiling meanly I thought how I intended to make my Canadian prince stew a bit, cook him a bit more and more before I allowed him to shoot that pent-up load of ball juice...

When Dave's hole was as wet as a duck's bottom and dripping with a mixture of sweat and my saliva I stopped working it... for the moment... I sat up on the bed, grabbed Dave's upturned socked calves and began trailing the tip of my tongue up and down the backs of his legs and thighs, slapping them and pinching them a bit for fun as I went.

Dave grunted and swore like a captured marine as I trailed my lips and tongue over the backs of his legs, thighs and even over his sweet melon-shaped ass cheeks.

"OHHHH, delightful," I mused as I trailed my way back up the backs of his legs and thighs, tweaking his wet asshole with a finger or two in between just to make his head spin all the more.

"OH Chris, yes, delightful is the word, I feel like I can cum just from what you're doing to me here," Dave squawked, writhing in his bonds at that point. "My cock is SO hard and throbbing like a jack hammer..."

"Not yet Dave, not yet," I said in a commanding tone of voice. "Not yet..."

"I-I'll do my best Chris," Dave stammered and then shrieked as my tongue found its way to his visible scrotum between his upturned legs. "OOOOOOOOOOO..."

I licked and slathered my tongue over and over the underside of Dave's sac, from that position able to look down into his handsome face as I worked him over... and over...

"OH MY, I love what you're doing to me now Chris, that feels so good," Dave cried, his eyes squeezed shut as I licked and kissed his balls.

His hard cock twitched and danced between his legs as I did my work on his testicles, holding onto the backs of my Canadian prince's thighs as I did so...

I dribbled a goodly amount of saliva all over Dave's scrotum and sucked it up, sucking his testicles alternately in and out of my moth as I did so.

"Too much now, too, too much, oh my, this is over the top," Dave panted breathlessly. "Please let me cum Chris, please..."

Dave loved what I was doing to him and I loved the sound of Dave pleading; I loved the sound of him saying my name as his passion ignited more and more. It was like a drug I could not get enough of, Dave was like a drug I could not get enough of...

When I saw that his cock would erupt any second I knew that I couldn't make the Canadian prince hold out much longer, his need to cum was beyond intense at that point. I stopped licking and kissing the backs of his legs and thighs and scurried off the bed.

"WH-what are you doing?" Dave asked. "Please Chris, please, don't leave me hanging like this... OH MY, I need to cum..."

"And I have just the thing to help you along bud," I stated and for the last time that day reached into my backpack. "I have just the thing you love oh so much..."

That said I held up the vibrating butt-plug that I had used on Dave in our role-play session.

"OH MY WORD..." Dave thundered as I clicked the buzzer on and aimed it at his asshole.

"Good thing I saliva lubed you huh Dave?" I teased him, rubbing the tip of the device against his ass walls before inserting it inside him.

"OH YES, yes, you lubed me real nice with your sweet saliva Chris," Dave panted crazily. "Now please, please... let's get this show on the road... as the saying goes..."

"Yes, as the saying goes," I repeated to Dave, smiling lovingly at him and slowly slid the vibrating butt-plug into his anal canal.

"AAARRRRRHHHH, yes, oh yes," Dave shrieked joyfully and bucked in his tight bonds. "OH that is such an amazing feeling Chris, my USA stud, oh my word, and being tied up like this simply makes it all the more intense..."

I swiveled the buzzing device around and around in Dave's hole and I nearly laughed my head off as Dave's eyes spun a bit in his head at the same time.

"OOOOOOOO, oh my fuck," Dave swore. "I-I'm gonna cum without my cock even being touched, this is just TOOOOOO over the top now, and I swear, I'm over the top as well..."

Then, Dave curled his toes back in his sweat socks, curled his fingers into big fists and shot his load all over his chest area, stomach region and onto his nipples...

"AWWWWWWW... yeah, oh Chris, Christopher, my USA stud, how you know how to play me," Dave seethed through clenched teeth as he spurted and spewed his mess of Canadian slime all over himself, a veritable feast.

I jammed the butt-plug further inside Dave till it hit home and he let out another loud shriek of passion and still more thick slimy ropes of sperm erupted from his wide sexy cock slit.

"AWWWWWWWWW..." Dave groaned like a madman at that point.

When he was done I slowly slid the butt-plug out of him, not wanting to torment his now very sensitive asshole, seeing as the man truly had suffered enough for one day. Once the plug was out of his hole Dave begged his usual mantra of me, pleading, "Untie me, please, untie me now Chris..."

I quickly did as Dave asked, wanting him to know that he could trust me, no matter how much I had just tormented and teased him... plus, I wanted to feast on the load he had just provided for me. I got up off the bed and untied Dave's raised socked feet first, peeling his sweat socks off him as well, just for fun, and then untied his wrists from the bed board.

Once he was untied Dave stretched himself out on his bed and panted anew and writhed in afterglow ecstasy as I quickly stripped myself naked, laid over him on the palms of my hands and the toes of my feet and licked and ate his creamy cum off his chest, his pecs, his stomach area and sucked it heartily off his delectable nipples.

"My God Chris, OOOOOOOOO..." Dave gasped breathlessly and this time there were tears in my eyes.

"Oh Dave, you make me so happy," I said and when he saw the tears flowing down my face he sat up and gathered me into his muscular arms.

"Hey, no tears bud, no tears huh?" Dave asked me softly, pressing his lips against my cheek and kissing me as he held me close against him, leaning his back against the bed board.

"These aren't tears of anguish my Canadian prince, they're tears of joy," I replied and adored this man even more as he sucked his cum that had accumulated on my lips into his mouth and gulped it down.

We both chuckled and he kissed my cheek again.

"If you must know, I LOVE the things you do to me, your games, your torments, it's all new to me, and so exciting Christopher," Dave whispered into my ear... and then... to my TOTAL surprise, he grabbed my hard cock tight.

"OHHHHHHHH..." I grunted as my Canadian prince squeezed and twisted my erection.

"Tie a guy up while he's taking a power nap Chris?" Dave teased me, feigning anger as he began stroking my erection, holding me tight with one arm around me. "I have to say that that's a pretty shitty thing to do to a poor guy huh?"

"YES, yes, if you say so Dave, if you say so," I panted.

"Well guess what my USA stud? Your Canadian prince isn't tied up now," Dave seethed in my ear, biting my earlobe a bit as he went on stroking me, milking me, fixing to get a load or two it seemed out of me.

"NO, no, you're not," I gasped and then after a few more good hard strokes Dave pumped a potent load out of me, me grunting and groaning and the one swearing like a captured marine this time.

"Oh yes my USA stud, shoot that load, shoot that load for me," Dave demanded.

"Oh yeah," I was seething now. "Tying you and teasing you really gets me off Dave."

"So it does, so it does," Dave said and when I was done he gave my slimy sensitive cock a few last tugs, making me shiver against him.

"So, you sure you're not mad at me my Canadian prince?" I asked Dave and picked up a length of the rope from the bed that I had used earlier to tie his feet with.

Dave kissed the back of my neck, disentangled himself from me and said, "How could I POSSIBLY be mad at you my USA stud?" and to my shock held his wrists tightly together in front of himself.

I smiled meanly, began twining the length of rope around my Canadian prince's wrists and said, "This time I am going to blindfold you," and we both laughed, anticipating round two that day...

Definitely not The End...

Dave, In His Red and White Speedo Scene

After his hard and grueling workout that morning Dave was in a deep sleep. The older mature beyond handsome Canadian gentleman took pride in the fact that he kept himself in such great and muscular well-toned shape. And always, after his punishing workouts at the gym Dave liked to relax with what he called a power-nap, which was essentially what he was doing at the moment, power napping, yes, he was in a deep sleep, that was until he felt the flicking of a tongue on the outline of his big testicles as he lay on his bed in just a pair of his prized red and white Speedo and left over thick white calf-length sweat socks.

The handsome older man stirred slightly on the bed and smiled through pursed lips as he slowly came awake, slowly climbing up and out of the land of slumber, out of the arms of sleep.

"Mmm…" he murmured contentedly, him knowing who it was that was lovingly and erotically licking his family jewels through his silk Speedo.

As Dave slowly opened his eyes, lying on his back on the bed, he looked down and saw…

"Christopher," Dave said, sounding a bit husky with sleep still. "I'm so glad I gave you a key to my place bud, but aren't you a bit early for our brunch date my special buddy, my sexy Speedo eating USA stud?"

As Dave spoke the sounds of his sexy voice sent chills up Christopher's spine.

The younger man gripped Dave's well-toned thighs, caressed them lovingly and then licked the outline of Dave's steely erection that was still encased in his Speedos, getting a few sexy sounding moans out of the Canadian prince.

"Yeah, I suppose I'm a bit early for our brunch date," Christopher chuckled as he looked up at Dave's gloriously handsome smiling face. "But I wanted an appetizer and then some before we went out."

"So you did, so you did," Dave said, smiling broadly now as chills slid through his being, as his buddy once again devoured him. "Ohhhh… and as always what you're doing and the way you're loving me is intensely sensual and… and…"

But then, as Dave attempted to stretch out and move his muscular arms he realized that they were shackled at the wrists to his bed board behind him. He looked upward and saw that his arms had been stretched tight above his head and that his wrists were locked in leather wrist restraints which were hooked up to his bed board.

"Oh God Christopher, *Oh God*, you've done it to me again bud," Dave grunted as now more intense feeling chills coursed through him as Christopher ate his Speedo covered crotch in a faster tongue flicking motion. "...tied me up again!!"

Dave was bellowing in a mixture of alarm and ecstasy, trying it seemed like he was deciding whether he was ecstatic or pissed off over what his special buddy had done to him, and while he was sleeping no less.

"I have to say again Dave, you sleep beyond soundly after you've worked out really hard, you should realize by now how dangerous that can be for someone like you, when someone like me loves tying you up just for the fun of it," Christopher teased and planted a few hard kisses on the throbbing bulge in Dave's silk Speedo.

"OOOHHHHH..." Dave moaned. "Never knew anyone in my life before who loved tying me up the way you do Christopher, that is for sure..."

"You didn't even stir as I got you locked to your bed board this time buddy," Christopher said and resumed licking the outline of Dave's cock and balls in his Speedo.

Then, just to be a tad mean Christopher pulled the drawstring on Dave's Speedo tighter, causing the garment to really hug the handsome older man's crotch and ass areas, really making his private parts all the more sensitized feeling as Christopher worked his magic on them.

"OHHHHH... and I can just imagine what tricks you have up your sleeve for me this time," Dave huffed as Christopher literally devoured his Speedo covered crotch area.

"Oh yes Dave, many new surprises are in store for you my buddy, my Canadian prince," Christopher replied, sounding as fiendish as possible.

Christopher slid down a few inches, gripped Dave's sexy muscular thighs and buried his face in the older man's Speedo covered crotch, inhaling the musty manly scent emanating from there.

"OHHHHH nice," Dave moaned as he stretched himself out tighter on the bed as he was ravished.

The Canadian gentleman arched his head back a bit and looked up at his wrists locked in the leather restraints and hooked to his bed board.

"Tell me to undo the restraints Dave, that's all you have to do, you know that," Christopher said, holding his buddy's thighs and grinning up at him.

"N-no," Dave whispered. "Don't set me free Christopher, not now, not now…"

Christopher chuckled meanly, kissed the bulge in Dave's Speedo a few times and then started snaking his way down the older man's thighs, kissing them as he went, licking them, sending chills through Dave, making his head spin…

"OHHHHHH, this is heaven, pure heaven my USA stud," Dave swooned and straightened his head back out, watching as his sinister buddy devoured and loved him in his special erotic way.

"That's a good boy Dave, and you know having you tied up makes all of this a whole lot better, and since you're wearing just your Speedo," Christopher teased and in a quick motion yanked Dave's calf length thick white sweat socks off his feet, tossing them to the floor, the scent of Dave's manly sweaty feet filling the air. "… I can now massage your thighs and your calves and your feet, oh yeah, doesn't that all just feel oh so good my Canadian prince?"

As Christopher spoke he kneaded his way down Dave's muscular sexy legs, until he got to his bare feet and massaged and squeezed the fuck out of them, loving the moist feel of them in his fingers.

"OHHHHHH Christopher, oh man, oh God, this is... ohhhhhhh....if I didn't know better I would swear you have gone and totally seduced me with your erotic wiles," Dave moaned. "Yes, I do want you to untie me, but at the same damned time, I DON'T want you to untie me... Oh God, Oh God... But, but even though I'm tied up again... I know you won't hurt me, right? You, you have said you love me after all..."

And as Dave spoke and as Christopher sucked one of his big toes the Canadian gentleman's cock throbbed in his tight, tight Speedo.

"Oh my Canadian prince, you are so befuddled," Christopher teased his prize. "I have made you a changed man, a man who loves to be tormented and teased, but yes, you are in total control, sort of, hee, hee, hee... remember, even though I am the one who has YOU tied up and secured I am still powerless against the attraction and the desires I feel for you... and Dave, those desires include making you crazy..."

"OHHHHH," Dave groaned louder and his hard cock throbbed even more intensely as Christopher sucked one of his big toes.

"I-I feel so swimmy headed, OHHHH, please, take my Speedo off me bud, I want my cock freed, please, I want to be completely naked for you Christopher... OH, what have you done to me man? It does feel so good you sucking on my toe like that, never thought that could feel so good,

so good that I feel it in my trapped cock in this Speedo...
please... take this Speedo off me Christopher..."

"Now, now Dave, just relax, hee, hee, hee, you know
that part of the allure of you is you wearing those Speedos
of yours that you love so much, and that I LOVE seeing you
in," Christopher laughed and quickly slurped Dave's toe
back into his mouth, massaging and kneading the Canadian
prince's sweaty naked foot at the same time.

"YES, yes, love wearing Speedos," Dave moaned
in reluctant agreement. "I'll, I'll endure it buddy, for you
Christopher, awwwwwww... feels so good... anything for
you Christopher..."

Once more Christopher released Dave's toe from his
mouth, held his naked foot tight and looked down at Dave,
smiling devilishly, "Yes Dave, yes my Canadian prince, my
submissive handsome man, you know that I am the Master
of your universe at the moment, and I am titillating that
universe through one of your toes... you know that I'm in
control here, don't you Dave?"

"OH yes, oh my, Christopher is in control," Dave
muttered through quivering lips. "And, and my cock is so
hard... and my balls are aching... WHAT???"

"Dave, when I have you tied up and under my
control I crawl into your head, and I am like an octopus,"
Christopher whispered and slithered his tongue up and
down the bottom of Dave's foot, kissing it a few times as
well. "I am not limited by just having only two hands, two
arms and one mouth my Canadian prince, I can plant the
seeds of what I am doing into your psyche and really make
you nuts, I'm like many Christopher's working on you at the
same time. I can lick your feet, suck your toes, chew on your
tits, eat your anal canal, I can do it all, edge you and dangle

you over a cliff and make you beg me to let you cum… and I won't… your need to cum will be ASTRONOMICAL… and I locked your pesky hands away so that you would not get any ideas of getting yourself off bud."

As Christopher spoke and squeezed Dave's foot and licked it and kissed it Dave squirmed miserably and in ecstasy…

"In my psyche?" Dave asked and suddenly, Dave didn't even notice that Christopher had moved, his buddy was laying partially atop him… and sucking hard on of his jutted up sensitive nipples. "OH MY WORD, sucking my tits now… What is going on… what have you… oh my Christopher, my USA stud, you are everywhere… oh, I feel it even more now in my hard cock… oh please… please take my Speedo off me and free my hard cock…"

"I really am so glad that you sleep so soundly after you work out my Canadian prince," Christopher teased poor Dave even more then as he sucked one of the guy's nipples and tweaked and twisted the other one at the same time. "Oh my sexy and pumped up Dave, what has happened to your fetish to be wearing that silky sexy Speedo? No, I'm not taking it off you just yet bud, I have too many more things in mind to do to you… but not to worry, at some point before this day is over I will drain your balls dry… but I am so thrilled that you have once again fallen prey to my seductive ways…"

With that Christopher squeezed and twisted one of Dave's nipples hard with his fingers and thumb and slurped and sucked and nursed on his other nipple like a madman at the same time…

"OOOOOOOO, oh please Christopher, PLEASE…" Dave thundered then, arching his head back once more and looking up at his wrists in the shackles. "You are TRULY making me insane here... You have done it to me again bud... and yes, I have fallen prey to your seductive ways once more, and I have to say that I'm just too happy to be your victim once more... you truly have DONE IT to me again..."

"And I plan to continue doing it to you... bud..." Christopher chuckled meanly.

Dave straightened his head back out and watched in awe and his sexual ecstasy reached new heights as his USA stud alternately sucked his nipples, and while he sucked one nipple Christopher made sure to be squeezing and tweaking the tar out of the other one, never for a moment offering Dave any relief or release as his nipples became the control knobs for his hard throbbing cock trapped in his tight Speedo...

After a half hour of truly working Dave's nipples Christopher stopped and reached into his backpack.

"Oh no, what now?" Dave murmured. "What all do you have in that notorious bag of tricks of yours that you plan to use on me... OH SHIT..."

Smiling evilly Christopher held up a pair of alligator teeth tit clamps...

"No wonder you sucked and slurped and squeezed my tits up to twice their size," Dave cried, squirming in his bonds as Christopher squeezed the tit clamps open. "OH, but Christopher, you said you would never hurt me. Won't those clamps hurt once you clip them to my tits???"

"Just for a moment or so my Canadian prince," Christopher replied and then he was holding the open tit clamps around Dave's nubs, making the guy anticipate the coming sting. "But once they're on and hugging your tits your cock will love it... it's when I take them off you later, much later, that you'll be screaming so loud I may have to gag you... Hee, hee, hee for you my buddy..."

With that, Christopher snapped the tit clamps onto Dave's nipples, encasing the guy's beefy nubs in them...

"ARRRRRRHHHHH, oh you fucker," Dave reeled and twisted on the bed real sexily. "Why oh why do I allow you to do these things to me Christopher??? I was so vanilla before I met you and... OOOOOOOOOO"

But then, the feelings of pain in his clamped nipples was replaced by a feeling of sexual hyper-sensitivity as Christopher then moved down back to Dave's crotch area and began once more swirling his tongue over the Canadian's Speedo covered crotch.

"RRRRRRRRR... OH MY GOD..." Dave grunted through clenched teeth and clenched his bound hands into fists.

Christopher swirled and trailed his tongue over and over and over the outline of Dave's cock and balls in his tied tight Speedo, sending his Canadian prince to even higher heights.

"OH MY WORD, my head is beyond swimmy feeling now Christopher, I swear I could cum just from what you're doing to me bud," Dave seethed. "OH MY poor tits... my poor goddamned tits."

Being the mean guy that he can be at times Christopher reached up to Dave's nipples, grabbed the short chain that was attached to the tit clamps and gave it a few gentle pulls...

"ARRRRRRRRRR!!!!! OH, that is a shitty thing to do to a guy that you claim to love Christopher!" Dave ranted as his tits felt as if they were literally on fire.

Christopher kissed Dave's crotch area, marveled at how the guy's pre cum was oozing through the thin material of his Speedo and tugged again on the tit clamp's chain…

"YUHHHHHHH!!!!" Dave snarled and rested his head atop his stretched out arms, watching intently as Christopher playfully licked up the pre cum that continued to ooze through the thin material of his Speedo.

"You know I do love you Dave," Christopher whispered. "If I didn't love you I wouldn't be so anxious to do these things to you… let's just say you bring out the beast in me."

With that Christopher kissed the outline of Dave's cum stuffed balls through the thin material of his Speedo.

"OOOOOOOOOO, oh yes, oh yes," Dave moaned and groaned, resting his head atop his stretched out arms.

"And you know that all you have to do is say the word and I'll untie you Dave," Christopher said and a look of alarm filled Dave's beautiful eyes.

"NO, NO, don't untie me Christopher, please, don't untie me, not yet at least bud," Dave panted pleadingly, not believing himself the words that were coming out of his mouth.

The sounds of Dave not wanting to be freed was music to Christopher's ears and he gently kissed the outline of Dave's testicles in his Speedo over and over, whispering Dave's name over and over as he did so.

"I know Christopher, I know, I feel it too," Dave gasped, watching as his buddy kissed and licked his balls, and taking in the sight of his clamped up nipples. "Believe me my USA stud, I feel it TOOOOOO…"

Then, Christopher slowly undid the drawstring in Dave's Speedo and hooked his fingers around the sides of the skimpy silk garment.

"Oh yes, yes," Dave marveled happily as Christopher slid his Speedo slowly down his sexy muscular legs and off him, tossing it aside.

Dave's big cock sprung up hard as a flagpole and oozed and dribbled massive amounts of dollops of pre cum.

"OHHHHHH feels so good, I do love wearing Speedos as you know, but I also love how hard my cock gets in them as well bud, and with what you're doing to me at the moment, my cock sure is HARD my USA stud," Dave panted and then let out a screech as Christopher took his cock by the tip only in his fingers, leaned down and slathered and tongue bathed his now naked balls. "EEEEEERRRRHHHH, OH MY GOD, having my tits clamped somehow makes that feel all the more... MORE..."

"Yeah, I'll agree bud, a guy's tits sure are his highway to heaven," Christopher laughed meanly in between licking and lapping Dave's sweaty testicles and pinching the tip of his pre cum oozing hard cock and from the sound of Christopher's voice Dave knew that his buddy's sinister side was rearing its head yet again...

A short while later Dave found that he had been VERY correct; as Christopher's sinister side had indeed reared its head yet again, it was a beautiful head Dave thought but sinister nonetheless as the Canadian gentleman now found himself in a most heinous of positions yet again... just like the last time Christopher had managed to get the drop on him by tying him to his bed board while he had been sleeping... Christopher now had Dave in a halfway folded up position, as now, not just Dave's wrists were tied to the bed board but his feet, due to the fact that his legs had been widely spread and pulled apart to expose his anal canal were also tied up to the bed board as well, with mounds of rope wound around and around his ankles, the bottoms of his naked feet looking up at the ceiling.

"OOOOOOHHHH God, you sure do love doing this to me Christopher," Dave panted as he squirmed somewhat miserably in his bonds as his USA stud was just finishing tying up his left foot as he stood on the side of the bed that had become Dave's sexual prison.

Before stepping away from Dave's now bound up foot Christopher slurped the big toe of that foot into his mouth, gripped Dave's foot real tight at the arch and center and sucked his big toe as if it was a dick, swirling and twirling his tongue around and around and over it at the same time.

"OOOOOOOO, that feels so good Christopher," Dave reeled; I swear I can feel that in my clamped tits, my hard cock and my aching balls. "You sure do know how to torture me in such a loving way bud…"

Holding Dave's foot in two hands then, massaging it a bit, Christopher stared down at Dave, a dreamy and lust-filled loving look in his eyes.

"Dave, you cannot know just how much it means to me to see you this way," Christopher whispered.

"I do get that my USA stud," Dave replied with a grin and Christopher let go of his foot, stepping to where his backpack, his bag of tricks as Dave called it was.

Seeing Christopher pick up his backpack and reach into it, Dave asked, "So uh, now that you have me this way, what all are you planning on doing to me next my USA stud?"

Christopher smiled devilishly and said, "I really should get into the habit of blindfolding you bud, not only does it make the suspense of what I'm going to do to you all the more riveting when I do it, but you really do look so sexy and vulnerable to my wishes when your beautiful peepers are covered with a silk cloth.

"Well, seeing as I'm tied up and tit clamped at the moment I would say that I am glad I am not blindfolded as well," Dave laughed and his eyes opened wide in a mixture of ecstasy and curiosity when he saw that Christopher took a thin leather cock ring from his bag along with a thin leather length of cord as well. "Oh my, what all are you planning on doing with those items my USA stud?"

Still smiling devilishly Christopher sat down on the bed on his knees directly in front of Dave's upturned ass. Without a word he arranged Dave's balls so that they were dangling over his ass crack.

"OHHHHHH, love it when you handle me like that bud," Dave swooned as Christopher yanked down a few times on his buddy's testicles, causing Dave's hard cock to stick straight up like a birthday candle in the dead center of a cake.

"Okay, your balls are hanging nice and low, perfect for a cock ring bud," Christopher chuckled and putting aside the thin leather cord (for the moment) he dutifully snapped the cock ring around the base of Dave's balls good and tight.

"EEERRRHHHHHH, OH fuck, now my tits are really scorching Christopher, why in all hell is that???" Dave panted and twisted in his bonds.

"It's because every part of you is becoming more and more sensitized buddy," Christopher replied and gave Dave's cock ringed balls a few squeezes and tugs.

"OOOOOOOHHH, I'll say, and then some..." Dave breathed deeply. "GOD, my tits are sore..."

Leaning in closer to Dave Christopher began looping the thin leather cord around and around his bound up prize's hard cock-shaft... in a crisscross motion, starting at the base of the guy's cock.

"ERRRRRRRRRR," Dave seethed again. "OH MY COCK, OH MY TITS, OH MY BALLS, OH MY GOD my USA stud, you really know how to make me crazy," Dave cried in a mixture of ecstasy, anger and outright lust.

"Still not going to tell me to untie you my Canadian prince?" Christopher teased as he dressed Dave's cock in the leather cord; looping it up, up, up as he went.

"NO, no, I want to see where all this goes, because man, I can tell you, every time you tie that leather cord around my hard cock, I swear I can feel that I am about to shoot a load like NEVER before in all my goddamned life... my god-damned-OH MY FUCKS!!!!"

Dave roared then, and as Christopher tightened the cord around and around the crown area of his cock, the Canadian prince, did just that, shot his load like a madman. "OOOOOOOOHHHHHH..."

Smiling dreamily then Christopher gave the leather cord a few last squeezes around Dave's cock and as the man spurted, spewed and spit his load from his wide sexy slit he tied the ends together, fully encasing his buddy's cock in the leather device.

Resting his head against his bound up arms Dave ranted, reeled and screamed in a man's passion that he truly HAD NEVER felt before in all his years.

He squeezed his eyes shut and wondered how this USA stud had been able to make him into the kinky man he now was, when all he could remember before Christopher was being oh so vanilla, except for his Speedo fetish that is, which seemed tame now compared to the things he was allowing Christopher to visit upon him…

"OOOOOOOOOOHHHHH," Dave howled and writhed atop the bed as Christopher finished tying the ends of the leather cord together at the tip of his still hard cock. "TH-that was monumental my USA stud…"

"And we're still not done yet my Canadian prince," Christopher laughed meanly as Dave spurted the last of his mess from his cock onto his stomach region.

"AAAAWWWWHHHH, oh fuck, oh Christopher, my tits, they're burning up in those clamps now, they feel like they're stinging and zinging me, they are on fire bud!!"

"And to add to your misery my sexy prisoner, now that your cock is tied up the way I have it you won't lose that erection all too soon either," Christopher said and slid a finger meanly into Dave's exposed asshole.

"YUHHHHHHHHH… OH MY WORD, like you said before, I feel like you got me balanced on the edge of a cliff here, I'm tingling everywhere bud and feeling like I could fall any second," Dave crooned and his head spun.

"Well, you know that after a guy shoots his load every part of him becomes all the more sensitive my Canadian prince, especially his tits and cock… and his asshole," Christopher said, wiggling his finger around and around in Dave's rectal opening.

"EEEEEERRRRHHH, true that my USA stud," Dave seethed through clenched teeth and curled his toes back and forth a few times.

Christopher laughed meanly, slathered his tongue up the back of one of Dave's legs, sending chills through him and slowly and methodically slid his finger out of the handsome older man's hole…

"Now Dave, I have a REAL surprise for you," Christopher said, reaching for his backpack.

"OH my, and I can only imagine what it is," Dave panted, sweating now in his bonds.

"Trust me, you have no clue what I'm about to do to you my Canadian prince, but I will say this, you are about to cum… AGAIN…" Christopher said, sounding almost threatening as he reached into his backpack.

"C-cum again?" Dave panted. "So soon???"

Then, Dave's eyes opened wide in disbelief as Christopher held up a small blue pill.

"Wh-what is that Christopher?" Dave asked. "You know I don't do drugs of any kind…"

"Not to worry my Canadian prince, this is a potent enhancer from the Orient," Christopher chuckled.

"An enhancer? You mean Viagra?" Dave asked, still reeling in a mixture of pain and ecstasy.

"As close to it as one can get," Christopher replied and to Dave's total shock and disbelief Christopher slid the tiny pill into his exposed asshole.

"ULLLLLPPPPP… what in all hell???" Dave blanched and as he wriggled on the bed in his bonds he could not believe how he felt his asshole literally suck the little pin in.

"And once that takes effect and you cum again I'll take the tit clamps off you Dave," Christopher said, getting to his feet and beginning to undo the ropes around Dave's left foot. "And when those tit clamps come off you'll begin a whole new career, as an opera singer… Hee, hee, hee for you again my very special buddy…"

"T-takes effect?" Dave asked incredulously.

"Yeah, you should feel it in a few minutes," Christopher said as he lowered Dave's now untied left foot down to the bed.

"Opera singer??? Oh no, my poor tits, my poor, poor tits, Dave whimpered.

And then, a few minutes later, Dave lay spread out on the bed, his legs now wide open and his naked ankles tied with mounds of rope, the slack of the rope tied off to the legs of the bed...

"OOOOOOHHHH, oh my word, I am feeling it again, I am so horned up Christopher," Dave panted, sounding delighted in his bound up helplessness. "OH MY FUCKS, I feel like I can shoot my load again... and again... and again... oh my, what exactly was that stuff that you just fed me through my asshole man???"

Christopher chuckled and said, "I told you, it was an enhancer, and you shall cum again my Canadian prince."

With that Christopher tightened the cock ring on the base of Dave's balls and undid the leather cord around his throbbing hard cock, freeing the man's shaft...

"OH MY BALLS," Dave grunted as goose bumps broke out all over his well-toned muscular body. "I love it when you handle me there Christopher... and... OOOOOOOO..."

Suddenly, Dave was swooning and spinning and his eyes rolled back in his head as Christopher gobbled his cock into his mouth, laying between Dave's spread legs, and sucking him for all he was worth.

"OOOOOOOOOO... oh my cock does feel oh so sensitive Christopher," Dave marveled at the feelings he was experiencing then. "I suppose between having cum already and having my tits clamped and having eaten whatever that pill was you gave me through my rear end... HOLY FUCKS, I am in total hyper-ecstasy here...

Christopher's head bobbed lovingly up and down on Dave's cock, sliding the entire length of it deep into his throat and swirling his tongue around and around it as he slid it back up into his mouth. When Christopher's face pressed against Dave's pubic bush and he tugged on his cock ringed balls the Canadian gentleman let out a howl, thus Christopher's prediction of Dave being an opera singer was realized at that moment...

"OOOOOOOOOHHHHH, OH MAN, I am cumming again, oh Christopher, I am cumming again..." Dave shrieked and shot his second potent load, right into Christopher's mouth.

As he bucked on the bed and struggled madly in the tight bonds he fed Christopher mouthful after mouthful after mouthful of his cock juice.

"UUUUUUUHHHH, this is just too unbelievable," Dave panted, his fingers twining and untwining as it seemed to him like it just would never stop as he shot still more of his good stuff, watching through tear-filled eyes as Christopher swallowed and gulped down every drop. "Oh my USA stud, my Christopher, my fucking hot stud..."

When he was finally done Christopher allowed Dave's shriveled cock to slide out of his mouth, smacking his lips around it as it came, driving chills and thrills through Dave's being.

"OH MY, I feel like I'm floating," Dave whined, looking up and suddenly seeing Christopher standing over him, smiling most lovingly.

"Good thing you're tied down then huh Dave?" Christopher asked and reached down to the tit clamps on Dave's nipples. "Wouldn't want you floating away now would we bud?

"N-no, I suppose not, bud," Dave panted breathlessly and then screamed and shrieked anew when Christopher unclipped the tit clamps from his nubs. "EEEEERRRRRRHHH, oh my fucks, oh my poor tits!!!! It hurts more now than when you first put them on me man!!!"

"It's just the blood rushing back into them Dave," Christopher reassured his special buddy as he stepped to the end of the bed and began undoing the ropes around Dave's left foot, freeing him. "They'll be fine, I promise you."

"I know they will, I know they will, because I know you would NEVER let any real harm come to me Christopher," Dave said, watching as his buddy untied his right foot then, impatient at that point to finally be untied, wanting to wrap his USA buddy in his arms and simply hold him and caress him.

Christopher then unshackled Dave's wrists from the bed board and sat down on his Canadian prince's lap once he had sat up.

"Feeling good buddy?" Christopher asked as Dave hugged him tight against his chest and planted delicate kisses on his cheek, inhaling his sexy scent.

"Oh yes my USA stud, you sure do know how to work me over," Dave said and pressed his face against Christopher's cheek, letting his tears of joy flow as he kissed him again. "Only you can do these things to me bud, only you... only you have tapped into that part of me..."

Christopher's heart felt as if it would burst with joy as Dave held him close, kissed him on the cheek and cried tears of joy down his face. Christopher turned his head and the two men's lips met and they kissed long, hard and passionately. As Dave sucked Christopher's tongue into his mouth he encircled a hand around his USA stud's hard cock.

"I love the effect my being tied up and at your mercy has on you bud," Dave said and began slowly stroking Christopher's cock, Christopher moaning in a man's passion as he was slowly and methodically brought to orgasm...

A while later, instead of heading out for their scheduled date the two men fell asleep in each other's arms...

Still Definitely Not the End...

Timmy's Office

*Author: Christopher Trevor and Inspired by: IMs
from Timmy Backman and John in Florida*

"MMMMMMMM, yeah, MMMMM, fucking A... MMMMMM... oh fuck yeah," Tim Backman, Timmy to his closest friends and family, swooned and groaned as muscle bound Vince, the handsome African-American Tickle Master held him balanced by his upper arms, Timmy's hands lashed behind him at the wrists with white cotton rope... him leaning down to the side and French kissing and sucking on the tongue of his other buddy who had come to his office to surprise him that day, Christopher. "So glad you two decided to pay me this visit, MMMMMMM... rather than kidnap my sexy ass like you did in the past."

Smiling evilly and holding Timmy tight by his upper muscular arms and relishing in the sight of the handsome banker lawyer's tied up wrists, his wiggling finger, and especially the ring finger on Timmy's left hand, viewing Timmy's wedding band and wondering what the beautiful Stephanie, Timmy's wife would think if she could see her handsomer than handsome hubby now, Tickle Master Vince leaned in close, bent Timmy over a tad more so his lips could really reach Christopher's, who was a bit shorter than Timmy, and trailed the tip of his tongue up and down Timmy's ripped muscular and naked back.

"AWWWWWWW..." Timmy moaned loudly and pressed his dripping wet lips against Christopher's as the guy hooked a hand around Timmy's big neck and trailed his fingers through the soft hair back there, tears of joy and ecstasy in Christopher's eyes as Timmy kissed him over and over... oh so very hungrily at that. "What a day this turned out to be huh buds?"

From behind him Timmy heard Tickle Master Vince say, "Oh yeah, great day buddy boy, but I sure do like it better when me and Christopher kidnap you, hee, hee, hee..."

At the sound of that hee, hee, hee, Timmy's blood ran cold and seemed to sluice through his veins at what felt like thousands of miles per hour. Clad in just a pair of tight white briefs by Under Armor and pair of OTC navy blue nylon dress socks by Gold Toe, Timmy, through quivering lips panted, "But, MMMMMM... but in a way you two have kidnapped me again, fuck, just look at how you got me here in my danged office of all places, stripped of my power suit down to my skivvies and socks, dang, oh my word, always my danged dress socks... MMMMMMMMM..."

As Timmy spoke and prattled Christopher kissed him on the cheeks, under his eyes, on the tip of his nose, on his forehead and then sucked Timmy's tongue back into his mouth again.

"MMMMMMMMM..." Timmy groaned as his buddy seemed to literally be devouring him.

Behind him Vince squeezed and kneaded Timmy's upper arms at his biceps curls, teasing the banker lawyer with his tongue on his back, the back of his neck and the erection in his jeans pressing against Timmy's sexy bottom as he and Christopher worked him over.

"Good thing we locked your office door before we stripped you down to your sexy essentials huh my ticklish laddy?" Tickle Master Vince teased Timmy.

Inwardly Timmy detested the nickname "Ticklish Laddy", as it was the name that his tickle nemesis and fucked up so called buddy, Ronald, the man who had kidnapped poor Timmy from his own home a few years back now and subjected the boy to three days of relentless tickle tortures had coined him with. (See the book "Timmy's Ticklish Trials" for complete descriptions of Timmy's tickle abduction.)

Then, before Timmy could reply, the Tickle Master gripped a handful of Timmy's soft wavy brown hair and pulled him to him, face-first and off Christopher's mouth.

"I want some of this now," the Tickle Master decreed and reveling in the sight of Timmy's sweaty face, his dripping lips and tongue half out of his mouth, Vince took his turn and clamped his mouth down on Timmy's.

"MMMMMMM..." Timmy swooned anew as now Christopher stood behind him, his author buddy kneading Timmy's ass cheeks through his white briefs, Timmy's mammoth sized erection dripping pre seed like a banshee in those white briefs.

"AWWWW you guys," Timmy managed to murmur in between Vince kissing him ever so sweetly and strongly.

Timmy's erection then did a sexy dance all its own called "Twitch and Tingle" in his underpants as Christopher squatted down behind him, ran his palms up and down the banker lawyer's thin dress socks, and pressed his mouth against his butt cheeks, kissing them through the soft white fabric of his briefs.

"AWWWWWW, yeah," Timmy crooned breathlessly as Tickle Master Vince was then holding him tight by the chin as his tongue explored his mouth.

As Timmy was ravished at the mouth, his socked calves and butt cheeks he quickly recalled how it had started out as any other workday, him sitting in his office, clad in a navy blue pinstriped suit by Armani, and poring over reports and documents that needed approval or disapproval ASAP for his vice president, Mr. Bradshaw. A regular day like any other, until his secretary, Janet, called his direct office line and told him that he had two visitors out in the reception area. Timmy knew he had no appointments scheduled for that day, so curiosity got the better of him and he told Janet that he would be right out.

The handsome banker lawyer put away the confidential documents and stepped out of his office and to the reception area. When he saw his two buddies, Tickle Master Vince and Christopher standing there he nearly jumped out of his well-shined black lace-up wingtips.

"Well holy crap and tarnation," Timmy sang out happily at the sight of the two handsome men, two handsome men that delighted in tormenting him in the most heinous, most ticklish and most devious ways that anyone possibly could, and in his deepest heart of hearts Timmy loved the two men for it and then some.

His secretary watched from her desk as her dapper boss dashed over to the two men and it was the African American who got to Timmy first, literally throwing his gigantically muscular arms around him and hoisting him off the floor. He kissed Timmy wet and Bugs Bunny style on one cheek, shouted out, "My Timy be!!!!" and spun Timmy round and round a few times, Timmy's shoed feet dangling and swinging. The other guy, a handsome white gentleman with brown hair and brown eyes and of average height watched almost in awe as Janet's boss was spun crazily.

When the African American gentleman put Timmy down, Timmy straightened his tie, breathlessly said, "Oh my word, what brings you two to Atlanta?" and shook hands with both of them.

"Book business," the white guy said. "What else could it be?"

Timmy laughed and said, "Knowing you two I never know what all you may have in store where I'm concerned."

At that point Timmy turned to his secretary and introduced the two men, telling her that the bald but with a goatee African American gentleman with striking dark eyes in the tight jeans and black polo shirt was Vince.

And that the white guy with brown hair and brown eyes and dressed in slacks, a sports jacket and shirt with no tie was Christopher, an author buddy of his, adding that both men were from New York.

"It's very nice to meet both of you," Janet said, getting to her feet and shaking hands with the two men, it not lost on her at all that these two men were crazy about her handsome boss, just as she was. But Timmy being as handsome and dapper as he was this did not surprise Janet whatsoever.

As she shook hands with the two New Yorkers a feeling of jealousy she never knew before coursed through Janet's being. It was one thing to compete with Timmy

Backman's wife for his attention, but now having to compete with two men, well, that was certainly a horse of another color… totally.

"So while we were here on my book business Vince and I figured we would pay you a visit," Christopher said to Timmy, a definite sinister looking glint in his eyes as he said it. "Plus I've never seen your office where you work so hard buddy."

"Well now, I'm real glad you did stop by then," Timmy said, beginning to sweat a bit in his suit and as usual, grabbed his tie, tugged at it nervously and straightened it as well. "My uh, my office is just down the hall here, so you two can surely come on in and see it."

"Are you sure Timmy B?" the guy named Vince said. "You sure you're not too busy or uh, tied up at the moment?"

Timmy cleared his throat nervously and said, "No uh, I can spare you two some of my time, my uh, my VP doesn't need the reports I was working on for another hour or so… right Janet?"

As Timmy spoke he looked at Janet and fidgeted a bit.

"Right Mr. Backman, please show your two friends your office," she said, sounding sexy as all hell as she sat back down.

As the three men started down the hall toward Timmy's office Janet leaned over her desk and called out, "Would you like me to have some coffee and other refreshments sent in to you Mr. Backman?"

"Uh, no, thanks Janet, we'll uh, we'll be fine, I think…" Timmy called back and before the three men entered Timmy's office Timmy found himself again being hoisted by Vince, the Tickle Master, as was his proper title.

"Oh my word, never had such fancy treatment bestowed on me before Vince," Timmy said as Christopher opened the door to Timmy's office and Vince gallantly carried Timmy over the threshold of that office in the position of a groom carrying his bride.

When the door to Timmy's office slammed shut and locked was when his secretary began to plot...

"Wow, that secretary of yours out there sure has it bad for you my ticklish Timmy B," Tickle Master Vince said and pecked Timmy on the cheek as he held him aloft almost effortlessly it seemed, as Christopher began unlacing Timmy's wingtips as they dangled in front of him.

"Not as bad as Douglas has it for me," Timmy replied and he and the Tickle Master watched as Christopher slowly and sexily de-shoed Timmy's feet, exposing his sexy tootsies in his navy blue Gold Toe socks.

"And who pray tell is Douglas?" Tickle Master Vince asked as he set Timmy down on his socked feet as Christopher dropped Timmy's shoes to the floor.

"Don't give Douglas another thought," Timmy said and then Christopher reached for his tie as the Tickle Master helped him out of his suit jacket. "Oh my word, I don't think I need three guesses to know what you two came here for..."

It didn't take long before the horned up banker lawyer found himself stripped down to his tight fitting white briefs and OTC navy blue nylon dress socks... and was being ravished with kisses on the mouth by his buddy Christopher...

"AWWWWWW..." Timmy found himself moaning as he was kissed and did not do anything whatsoever to stop

Tickle Master Vince from tying his hands securely behind him, if anything he seemed to relish in the feeling of being tied, as his hard cock became evident in his briefs.

"Fuckin' Southern prince of mine," Christopher whispered breathlessly.

Timmy's thoughts then returned to the present as Christopher, still squatting behind him began to slowly peel his underpants off him, sliding them down, down Timmy's sexy muscular legs, over his knees, over his socked calves... till Timmy gingerly stepped out of them when they were pooled around his feet... all the while Tickle Master Vince had the banker lawyer's tongue in his mouth and was at the same time squeezing, twisting and kneading the handsome boy's nipples.

"UHHHHHRRRRRR..." was the sound Timmy made as he was kissed what felt like the kiss of death... or life if you so prefer.

The banker lawyer then nearly jumped out of his blue dress socks when he felt Christopher pry his sexy well-muscled ass cheeks apart and plunge his tongue between them.

"YUUUHHHHHHH..." Timmy bantered breathlessly and pulled his mouth off Vince's. "OH my word, Christopher, what all are you doin' to me back there buddy???"

Tickle Master Vince watched evilly as Timmy danced and gyrated on his socked feet as his asshole was eaten like it was a pussy, the Tickle Master continuing to work Timmy's nipples at the same time.

"OOOOOHHH best two buds a guy can ever hope for," Timmy swooned, leaned his head down and his forehead landed on one of Vince's huge shoulders.

The Tickle Master smiled caringly this time, caressed the back of Timmy's neck... and kissed the top of his head as the guy crooned and swooned in goose bumps...

Christopher flicked his tongue around and around in Timmy's hole, spit liberally into it a few times, sucked his saliva out of it and sucked on Timmy's ass walls as well. With his hands bound behind him Timmy could only wish that he could get to his hard and throbbing cock so he could get himself off... but Tickle Master Vince had made sure that the banker lawyer stayed balanced on a sexual edge...

A few minutes later Christopher and Tickle Master Vince had Timmy splayed out on his desk, on his back... Christopher stood behind Timmy holding the guy's legs up and over his head by his socked ankles... as the Tickle Master slowly extracted his hard cock from his jeans...

"OH MY WORD..." Timmy grunted at the sight of Vince's thick and lengthy manhood.

"HA, if Stephanie could see her man now," Tickle Master Vince laughed and slowly inserted his steely rod into Timmy's sopped hole, spearing him lovingly as he went.

"OH MY..." Timmy blurted and felt fuller and fuller with each inch of Vince's cock as it entered him. "AAARHHHHHHH..."

The Tickle Master gripped Timmy as well by his socked ankles and began a rhythmic thrusting in and out of his moist hole.

"OH man, Christopher, it feels like velvet in here," Vince gasped as Timmy's hole hugged his cock each time it slid inside him.

As Vince plowed inside him Timmy curled his toes back under his socks, clenched his teeth and squeezed his eyes shut... all in a man's passion.

Then, when Timmy opened his eyes it was Christopher thrusting his cock inside him and Vince standing over his head, holding his socked ankles aloft, offering Christopher easier entry in Timmy's back door.

"OOOOOOO… my word, didn't even realize you two cads had switched places," Timmy murmured breathlessly.

A short while later Timmy's hole was filled with Christopher's and Vince's cum offerings, as both men had spewed their messes inside him, but had not permitted the banker lawyer himself to cum… which was par for the course Timmy thought. He was always left feeling frustrated and on the edge, as his Master Doug used to decree to him.

Timmy cringed and seethed as the two men teased him by sticking their fingers into his cum sopped hole… before lifting him off the desk and untying his hands.

"Oh my, so what are you two doing for dinner tonight, after your book business that is?" Timmy asked as Vince handed him his underpants and he and Christopher watched as he climbed into them, wiggling real sexily as he pulled them up and on.

Timmy's hard cock oozed oodles of pre cum, staining the front of his white briefs, seeing as his two conquerors hadn't offered him the luxury of shooting his load. His asshole still felt as if there was a cock wedged in there and he shivered with the feeling.

"We were thinking that maybe we would have dinner with you Ticklish Laddy, in our hotel room at the Georgia Diamond," Tickle Master Vince said, grinning meanly as he tossed Timmy his suit pants.

"Or perhaps have YOU for dinner Timmy," Christopher added suggestively.

Smiling shyly and with his hands shaking as he held his suit pants Timmy panted, "I'll make my excuses to Stephanie, somehow I get the feeling I'm going to be sort of tied up before heading home tonight…"

All three men laughed raucously and a few moments later Christopher and Tickle Master Vince kissed Timmy a few times more on the lips, sucked his tongue, tweaked his nipples and were then heading out the door of Timmy's office, quickly closing it behind them, not wanting any passerby who might be in the hallway to see Timmy still in just his underpants and tall socks…

As the door to his office closed Timmy gasped breathlessly a few times, thanked the gods in heaven for bringing him two such kinky friends as Christopher and Tickle Master Vince and was about to climb back into his suit trousers… when his office door opened and his secretary, Janet, sauntered in.

"Mr. Backman, now that your two friends are gone I thought we would go over," Janet began and then halted in mid-sentence when she saw her handsome boss standing there in just his briefs and tall navy blue nylon dress socks, about to climb into his suit pants.

"Janet, I…" Timmy began but then saw the way that his secretary was looking at the bulge in his white briefs… and when she licked her lips slowly and hungrily Timmy dropped his suit pants back to the floor… and Janet dropped the stack of files that she had been carrying.

With his erection oozing massive sized droplets of pre cum in his briefs Timmy watched and panted breathlessly as his secretary locked his office door…

"Oh my," the banker lawyer whispered and his hard cock twitched in his briefs.

A short while later Timmy was standing as if planted and rooted to the spot in his office, his hands once more bound behind him, and with the length of rope that Tickle Master Vince and Christopher had left behind no less, and this time, to add to his erotic misery he was blindfolded, with his own burgundy silk power tie at that…

As he stood there gasping and grunting in sexual agony he felt his hard cock being extracted from his white briefs, through the fly opening…

"Oh my, oh my word…" Timmy whispered breathlessly and his toes curled back in his dress socks as his cock was engulfed in a sweet soft mouth and tongue caressed. "Oh holy crap, what a day this turned out to be…"

As his hard cock was sucked and slurped on Timmy felt long fingernails caressing his balls through his briefs. He felt the palms of sexy and petite hands running up and down his muscular thighs, squeezing them… as his cock was sucked harder yet.

"YUHHHHHHH…" Timmy bantered as his head spun and he did his best to remain balanced on his socked feet, his head thrown back and looking up in blindfolded darkness. "OH my, getting there… getting there now… those two buds of mine didn't let me cum… but now I'm about to… I'm… UHHHHH… on no, for the love of heaven, NO!"

Timmy suddenly felt his pent-up load retreating as his cock was taken from the velvety feeling mouth.

As he stood there feeling a mix of sexual helplessness and a longing he hadn't known in quite some time Timmy felt those petite hands stuffing his engorged and pre cum dripping cock back into his white briefs.

"AW no, no," Timmy begged. "Please, please... I need to cum..."

The banker lawyer tried and struggled in vain to get his hands untied, but as he did so he then felt his cock and balls being tied up, the rope being wound round and round the base of them over his briefs...

"OH MY, what in tarnation now???" Timmy seethed through clenched teeth, his cock and balls churning like mad.

That evening, as Janet was finishing up her work for the day and closing down her computer, two janitors, Pedro and Victor came in, wheeling a big supply cart filled with cleaning utensils.

"Good evening Janet," Pedro, an older muscular, salt and pepper colored haired Spanish gentleman from Puerto Rico said in greeting.

"Hi guys, how are you two doing?" Janet responded as she shucked her bag over her shoulder.

"Doing well Miss," Victor, a sinister looking Spanish guy from the Dominican Republic said in a heavy Spanish accent as he eyed Timmy Backman's sexy secretary, as she stepped out from behind her desk.

"Everyone gone for the day Miss?" Victor asked Janet, his dark eyes seeming to bore into her, making her uncomfortable and wanting to get away from him as soon as possible.

"Yes, everyone except Mr. Backman, he's uh, a bit tied up at the moment, so you can work around him I suppose," Janet responded and headed for the door. "Have a good night guys."

The two janitors watched as Janet scurried out of the office, they shrugged and started moving their supply cart down the hall.

When they reached Timmy's office Pedro opened the door and as the two janitors stepped inside they stopped dead in their tracks at the sight before them...

There sat Timmy Backman at his desk, clad in just his white briefs and tall navy blue dress socks. The banker lawyer's hands were tied tight in front of him, the slack of the rope extended downward and binding his socked feet as well. Timmy was no longer blindfolded with his tie, rather it was crammed in his mouth and a length of rope was tied over it, jamming it in place, effectively gagging the poor guy...

To add further insult to the banker lawyer's misery the two janitors took in the sight of his tied up bulge in his white briefs. The way Timmy's crotch was tied up and his erection beyond paramount was more than titillating to the two suddenly horned up janitors.

"RRRMMMFFFF..." Timmy screamed miserably as he struggled to no avail in the tight bondage that he had been mercilessly left in.

The two janitors looked at each other and grinned devilishly from ear to ear...

A few scant moments later, the janitor named Victor was carrying Timmy from his chair where he had been seated, through his office and toward the huge supply cart...

"Well, if I can't have Mr. Backman's sexy secretary, I'll take the next best thing, her boss, Mr. Backman himself," Victor said as he lugged the load of Timmy out of the office and toward the supply cart.

"HHHRRRRRMMMFFF..." Timmy bantered in the janitor's face as he was carried and the janitor simply pecked Timmy on his gagged mouth in response.

Behind Victor, Pedro followed, carrying Timmy's suit and shoes with him...

Then, Victor loaded Timmy into a vacant section of the supply cart and slammed it shut.

"RRRMMMFFFF..." Timmy screamed miserably, thinking how he was again going to miss an appointment with Tickle Master Vince and Christopher.

The End

Willie's Velvet Highway

Smiling evilly from ear to ear I effortlessly carried the lanky and over the top well-proportioned, sexy as all hell, Latin, dark skinned, dark eyed, totally smooth, totally hairless, and erotically beautiful thirty something year old dude named Willie toward the bedroom where we would get to play. And as I walked slowly, carrying him by his perfectly coconut shaped ass cheeks, squeezing the fuck out of them in my huge truck driver hands he looked down at me a bit despondently because after we had been paired up by drawing cards I told him that I planned to do just a tad more than just "play" with him. He gasped a bit as I hoisted him a tad higher and pried his ass cheeks apart a bit, inching my long fingers toward his velvet highway, oh, what a piece of ass this Latino dude had... and I had plans for it beyond his realm of understanding. As he gasped again, his handsome head thrown slightly back I wedged a few inches of the first two fingers of both my hands into his sumptuous hole, his warm and velvet highway.

As I tweaked my fingers around at the edges of his smooth and moist ass walls he looked down at me beseechingly, his semi hard cock pressing against my chest, already leaking with his sticky nectar. Leering meanly into his puppy dog eyes as we approached the bedroom I squeezed his ass cheeks even harder, FUCK, I had never had the glory of feeling a butt as exquisite as Latin Willie's. His skin was as soft as fine spun silk and his ass muscles were as hard as rocks in my big ham-sized mitts. I kissed his pointy as darts nipples a few times, bit them, suckled them and whispered up to him as he whimpered, that I had won first prize in the mating game that paired up the participants of the party he and I had attended. In between whispering to him I kissed, sucked, suckled, bit and kissed his pointy nipples again and again, causing the guy to whimper passionately, breathlessly. We had drawn matching cards at the game that paired up the party participants, a fucking spanking party no less. His name was Willie and when he had shown up at the party I nearly lost my mind at the sight of him, he was that exquisitely (a word I don't use all that often mind you) beautiful. And when he stripped down to just his red calf length socks and sat down before the festivities would begin... well, needless to say I was totally bowled over the edge. Let me explain, you see, at the spanking party, the host, a real good buddy of mine named Bob asks that all the guests remove their shoes at the door before fully entering his very spacious three bedroom apartment.

Now, mind you, all the guests comply, seeing as we are all spanking fetishists and Bob is gracious enough to host these parties every three months or so, so really, what is the big deal? The guy likes to keep his place clean, and I can definitely get my arms around that. Now, as I said, we all comply and take our shoes off before we fully enter the apartment, leaving our footwear by the door. However, some of the more kinky dudes will strip down to their socks and underpants, just to be more comfortable, or perhaps they are showoffs you can say, and for some of the guys I have to say that I am real glad that they choose to show off. In my opinion nothing is sexier than a handsome dude sitting around in his under shorts and socks, a real nice vulnerable, sexy look. But then there was Willie… and like I said, he blew my mind first with his beauty when he walked in the door… even fully clothed he took my breath away, that face of his was beautiful enough to stop traffic, but then, when he stripped down to just his socks, no shame whatsoever in sitting there clad so scantily, well, even I was a tad shocked I have to say. As aggressive a Top as I can be, upon arrival at Bob's spanking parties I simply take off my work boots and sit around in my sweat socks, jeans and tee shirt until we're paired off for play time, or to be more precise, spank time.

Anyway, the host, Bob, a total spanking fetishist who knew I had a fetish for spanking hot Latino guys saw the way I was looking at Willie as he sat down among us. Bob managed to pull me aside and he told me that Willie was a total submissive. I had never seen Willie at any of Bob's parties.

Bob told me that this was Willie's first time attending one of his spanking parties, but he had spoken with Willie and had gotten to know him on the internet. He told me that Willie had just moved to New York from the Dominican Republic. His being Dominican attested to why he was so beautiful, FUCK, but I adore Dominican guys. AND, according to Bob there wasn't much Willie would stop a good Top from doing to him, as long as he got that shapely ass of his beaten like a rug. Well, I decided that I was Willie's man.

When we got to the threshold of the bedroom where I would be spanking Willie, and then some, I stood at the arch of the room, looking at the bed. It was as if the bed was inviting me and my prize. On the floor on the side of the bed was a black round leather paddle, which would be the instrument of Willie's torture, and then some. When Willie and I had drawn the cards that paired us together I had ordered the naked but for a pair of thick red calf length sweat socks to collect the leather paddle from Bob the host's arsenal of spanking supplies and to place it in the bedroom where he and I would soon be playing.

As Willie picked up the leather paddle and padded on his socked feet with it to the bedroom where I would minister to his sexy, sexy, delectable ass cheeks and then some me and Bob looked at each other and smiled deviously. I mouthed the words "Thank You" and Bob simply nodded, continuing playing the card game that would pair up his other spank party participants. Obviously Bob had set the deck of cards in my favor so that Willie would be my spanking prize. Once all the other party participants had been paired up, Tops with bottoms as is appropriate at these galas, Willie standing next to me turned to head toward the bedroom where he had placed the leather paddle. I quickly grabbed one of his smooth skinned upper arms in a FIRM, tight grip, yanked him back to me and seethed at him, "I don't recall giving you permission to precede me Velvet Highway." His dark eyes suddenly filled with trepidation AND longing, Willie looked up at me in all my six feet tall huge truck driver muscularity and whispered, "Velvet Highway Sir?" With that I pulled him toward me so we were chest to chest, reached around him and grabbed two handfuls of the most delectable, delicious looking and feeling butt cheeks I had ever had the pleasure of grabbing onto, and I hoisted him easily up and off the floor.

"ULPPPPP," Willie gasped as his red socked tootsies left the floor and I began the tract toward the bedroom, what would be this sexy Latin dude's torture chamber, YES SIR and RIGHTY HO... his long legs dangling and slightly swinging as I carried him.

As I stood at the arch of the bedroom Willie lifted his arms and twined his hands around the back of my neck, trailing his long thin fingertips over the short hairs back there. I was glad to feel that his hands were trembling, that was good, and he knew who was in charge here. My fingers kneaded his ass cheeks as I lugged him into the bedroom and pushed the door closed behind me with one of my big size twelve black sweat socked feet. The sound of the door slamming shut was obvious torture to Willie as he squeezed the back of my big neck tighter, leaned down and planted a small kiss on one of my cheeks. I jostled the guy a bit, hoisted him a tad higher and as he looked down at me with pleading in his eyes I meanly said, "You can caress me all you want Velvet Highway, I'm still going to spank you and work you over like no one's business." He gulped in terror as I gently set him down on his socked feet.

"Sir..." Willie began but I quickly held up a hand, silencing him.

"KNEES!!" I snapped at him, really in his face as I seethed the word at him.

With his lips trembling Willie gave me a quick peck on the cheek and seconds later he was kneeling before me.

"Good boy, good fucking boy," I grunted and in a fast move shucked my tee shirt off and tossed it aside.

As Willie stole a look up at my massive sized truck driver chest and I was unbuckling my belt I roared down at him, "HEAD DOWN!"

Once more he did as he was told, looking down at my big black sweat socked feet as I got myself more comfortable for the task at hand. I yanked my belt out of the loops on my jeans and swung it hard over Willie's back, thrashing him a few times, whipping him with it.

"OOOOOHHHHH SIR…" Willie cried out, his back heaving with each blow I administered to it.

After a good ten belt whips to his back I ordered Willie to look up at me… he did… and his beautiful eyes were tear-filled.

"My God…" I whispered, looking down at him as he knelt there on his knees in front of me.

I tossed my belt aside along with my tee shirt and nearly lost it as the guy leaned back on his knees, his toes curling in his red socks as he did so.

"Fuck me hard boy, but I am going to make that sweet ass of yours as red as those socks you got on," I ranted down at him.

"Yes Sir, as you wish Sir," Willie replied and then I pointed at the button on my jeans. "Get busy…"

Willie reached up and with his fingers trembling he unbuttoned my jeans, pulled the zipper down and then slowly slid my jeans down my long muscular legs. I stepped out of them and kicked them aside; standing over the guy now in my sweat scented black sweat socks and a musty scented jockstrap. Willie looked up at me as I towered over him and the tears spilled from his eyes and slid down his cheeks.

"Are those tears of joy or tears of fear boy?" I asked Willie, reaching down, trailing a finger through his tears and then sucking his tears off my finger; he was delicious, delicious in every goddamned way.

"Both Sir," Willie responded and then I pointed at the round leather paddle and snapped my fingers.

Willie instantly grabbed the leather paddle and bolted to his feet in front of me. He held the paddle out to me in a ceremonious manner, offering it to me as if I was a god of some kind.

I meanly snatched the paddle from him, turned my back and sat down on the side of the bed...

Willie turned and looked at me, his beautiful lanky hairless chest heaving up and down. Smiling contemptibly at him I held up the paddle and gestured with my index finger for him to approach me... he did, slowly.

When he was standing over me I held the leather paddle up to his trembling lips and without having to be told to do so he planted a few delicate kisses on it.

"Damn, you sure as all fuck know this routine boy," I sneered at the guy.

Then, I hooked my arm around his waist and in a fast pull had the guy bent over my lap area.

"ULLLLPPP..." Willie gasped as he landed.

"Get that sweet velvet highway in the air for me boy," I ordered, rubbing the paddle against his ass cheeks.

Willie did as he was told and I spit a few times onto his ass cheeks. I watched as my saliva slid down them and into his velvet highway and then raised my leather paddle. I brought it crashing down HARD on Willie's ass cheeks...

WHAPPPP WHAPPPP WHAPPPP WHAPPPP was the sound that filled the air around us then as I swatted and thrashed the best looking pair of ass mounds that I had ever come across…

"OHHHHH MYYYYY…" Willie cried out, his toes pressing against the floor and his arms dangling as he lay over my lap.

WHAPPPP WHAPPPP WHAPPPP WHAPPPP WHAPPPP went my leather paddle, harder with each blow, causing Willie's delectable looking ass cheeks to suddenly twitch with a life all their own.

"Oh yeah, getting there already boy, got those ass globes of yours twitching and switching for me," I said and raised my paddle higher this time. "But we're going to go past limits here…"

With brute strength I brought the paddle down hard on Willie's ass cheeks, spanking them alternately. *WHAPPPP WHAPPPP WHAPPPP WHAPPPP WHAPPPP WHAPPPP WHAPPPP WHAPPPP WHAPPPP WHAPPPP* went the next ten swats, HARD, and on Willie's right ass cheek.

"OH PLEASE SIR…" Willie cried and his socked toes slid against the wood floor, causing his red socks to scrunch down a bit in the process, making him all the more sexy somehow, if the guy could become any more sexy that is.

"I tell you boy, I can do this to you all day," I teased the Latin dude meanly and gave his right ass cheek another ten hard swats. "And I just might at that…"

"OOOOOOOOOWWWWWWW…" Willie howled, lifting his dangling head a bit, gasping.

"Oh yeah, fried ass cheeks boy," I said meanly and then before I began administering to Willie's left ass cheek I rubbed the paddle over it a few times, just to prep him.

"Please Sir, please..." Willie crooned, his breath catching in his throat.

"Getting to it as fast as I can boy," I chuckled sadistically and raised the leather paddle high.

WHAPPPP WHAPPPP WHAPPPP WHAPPPP WHAPPPP WHAPPPP WHAPPPP WHAPPPP WHAPPPP WHAPPPP sang my leather paddle as it kissed and burnt the Latin dude's sexy left ass cheek, making Willie howl like a wolf, a wolf in pain that is...

"OH SIR, that wasn't what I meant, Willie cried out.

I gave his left ass cheek another ten HARD swats and then switched back to the right one, gave it twenty hard swats and then back to the left one and gave it twenty hard swats... and then swatted both his ass cheeks over and over in succession... until those brown ass cheeks of the Latin dude were the color of brown mixed with red.

"ARRRRRRRRR!!!!!" Willie screamed in a real man's pain as I swatted and thrashed and paddled the tar out of his delectable ass cheeks.

"Fucking ass made for being spanked," I seethed down at the guy as he was by then sweating over my lap.

I rubbed his VERY wounded ass cheeks with the paddle in a circular motion. Those ass cheeks twitched in anticipation.

And then... *WHAPPPP WHAPPPP WHAPPPP WHAPPPP WHAPPPP*...

"OHHHHHHHHH, my poor ass," Willie blubbered by that point, sniveling with his head down, tears streaming down his exotically handsome face, snot pouring out of his nose.

WHAPPPP WHAPPPP WHAPPPP WHAPPPP WHAPPPP...

"ARRRRRRRRRRR!!!!!" Willie reeled as I relentlessly paddled him.

A short while later Willie's ass cheeks looked as if he had sat down on a hot waffle iron, they were that red and that wounded... and I was far from done with him...

As Willie whimpered and cried like a schoolgirl I placed the leather paddle on the floor at my socked feet, reached across the guy's sweated back, and grabbed him by a handful of his black hair.

"AAYYYYRRRRRR!!!" Willie screamed as I pulled him up and off my lap by his hair. "OHHHHH SIR!!!"

I ordered the Latin dude to get my under shorts off me and to mount my cock, telling him that I was about to give him the pony ride of his life...

Standing there in front of me, wiggling real sexily and stupidly on his socked toes, crying and sniveling miserably the guy looked down at me in disbelief.

"P-pony ride Sir?" Willie asked me and moved his hands behind him to rub his stinging and tingling ass cheeks.

"HALT boy!!" I shouted up at him. "I don't recall giving you permission to rub the burn out of those ass globes of yours. Now, just do as I told you or I swear I'll tie those hands of yours real fucking tight!"

Willie's eyes opened as wide as saucers, he stammered out the words "Yes Sir" and leaned down to get my white briefs off me, leaving me in just my black sweat socks at that point. My big cock popped straight up, long, beefy and hard, ready to plow into Willie's velvet highway...

"Oh yeah boy," I muttered, grabbed the guy by his sexy as hell hips, hoisted him up a bit, grunted with anticipation, and slid him down slowly, so slowly onto my throbbing cock.

"OOOOOOOOO SIR," Willie crooned, tears flowing freely from his eyes as he curled his fingers gently around the back of my neck.

"OH man Willie," I gasped as his ass walls, his velvet highway hugged my cock. "FUCK, feels awesome in there boy…"

"Th-th-thank you Sir," Willie gasped gutturally, a perplexed look in his dark eyes as I began sliding him up and down my cock by his hips.

"Fucking beautiful guy you are Willie," I whispered, leaned forward and slurped one of those pointy as darts nipples of his into my mouth.

"OOOOOOOHHHHH," Willie sang loudly as my big cow tongue worked swiveling magic on his sweet teat. "Sir, Sir, Sir…"

Willie leaned down and kissed the top of my head as I hoisted him up to just above my pre cum dripping cock and then slid him back down on it, him gasping as I speared him again… my spit from earlier in his velvet highway sure as hell acted like a good lube…

As I did it again, hoisted the guy up and back down onto my big rod I took note of how his cock was hard as hell as well. I chuckled a bit and slurped his other tit then into my mouth.

"AAARRRHHHHH OH YES SIR…" Willie swooned now.

He caressed my earlobes and whispered the words, "Thank you, thank you," over and over and over again…

"OOOOOOOOOHHH fuck yeah, filling your damned velvet highway with my spunk you sexy fucking Latino guy," I seethed a short while later as I then held Willie jammed down good and tight on my hard cock as I shot my load like a madman. "FFFFUUUUCCCKKKKKK!!!!"

As I shot and shot my load inside him the beautiful Latino guy leaned over me, I held him by his hips as he kissed the top of my head, squeezed my earlobes and cried tears of joy.

"OH please Sir, me too, me too, I need to cum for you as well, please Sir," Willie pleaded as I grunted like a captured marine, continuing to spew my mess into him, feeling it as remnants of my cum slid out of the sides of his velvet highway.

"NOT YET boy, not yet, you got more spanking and torments to suffer first before I decide to let you cum," I seethed up at him as he sat shivering with goose bumps on my cock. "OHHHHHHHHH…"

"OH NO SIR, please Sir," Willie pleaded and when my cock was spent and began deflating inside the guy I slid him off me to his feet, quickly spun him around so that his back was to me and ordered him to reach down and grab his sexy socked ankles. Horny as he was and as much as he seemed to need to cum, he instantly did as he was told… and FUCK BUDs, but that ass of his now looked beyond incredible as it stared straight up and he held tight to his red socked ankles. What a fucking stroke of luck Willie was for me.

I grinned meanly and nearly insanely, squatted down behind the guy, grabbed the backs of his upper slender sexy thighs in a FIRM and tight grip with my truck driver sized mitts and used them to pry his wondrous looking ass globes apart, exposing his cum sopped "velvet highway…" At the sight of the inside of Willie's pink hole I nearly cried myself, tears of joy that is. I stuck out my tongue and plunged it as far as possible into the sexy as all hell Latin guys' "velvet highway." Willie gripped his socked ankles tighter and moaned loudly and in a man's ecstasy as I began licking and lapping at his ass walls. Oh man, it was sheer heaven and sheer rank inside the guy.

"OOOOOO SIR, SIR," Willie cried out gutturally as I sucked my cum out of his asshole, reclaiming what was mine in a way.

"YUHHHHHHHH!!!!" Willie garbled as I licked at his bunghole, making his head spin… and I swear dudes, even though I had just shot a whopper of a load into the sexy Dominican guy's hole I was already boning up again.

FUCK, all I had to do to get myself fully boned again was to spank the tar out of Willie's delectable ass cheeks again, more intensely though the second time around, HAR, HAR, and HAR and then plow his velvet highway again. I spit globs of my cum onto Willie's ass cheeks after having eaten it out of his "velvet highway." I did this over and over again, preparing a nice meal for my spanking prize…

A short while later, Willie's entire sexy smooth skinned body was goose-bump riddled as I had him standing practically at attention next to me… as I trailed my fingertips over my cum that was all over his brown/red ass cheeks. I held two and three of my cum slopped and ass chowder covered fingers to Willie's trembling lips and without having to be told what to do he sucked my cum off them, his eyes squeezed shut in ecstasy as he did so.

"Oh yeah boy, you really know this routine," I mocked him.

As I trailed my fingertips again over his ass cheeks I could still feel the heat from the leather paddled spanking I had administered to him.

"Oh man, I want to make sure this ass of yours doesn't cool down Willie boy," I murmured as he licked his lips, hungry for more of my cum as I held my fingers again to his lips.

He sucked my fingers into his mouth, clasped his thick WET lips around them and hungrily ate my cum off them. Watching his Adam's apple bob up and down as he swallowed my cum off my fingers was riveting too for some reason...

But then, after all my cum was cleaned off my fingers I stepped away from Willie, sat back down on the bed and gestured with one finger for him to once more splay himself over my lap.

With a look of anguish mixed with intense desire Willie did as he was told and then, once more, I was looking down at two of the most exquisitely shaped ass globes anyone had ever had the good fortune to meet... and beat.

With one of my big hands wide opened I caressed, squeeze d and grabbed handfuls of Willie's ass cheeks, digging into them with my fingers. He moaned and groaned with sounds of pleasure mixed with pain, as his ass cheeks were obviously still smarting from my earlier punishments of them. I grinned from ear to ear as he wiggled like a fish out of water across my lap. Then, I ordered him to pick up my leather paddle, kiss it three times and then hand it up to me. My spent cock tingled as I watched the sexy Latin dude once more do my bidding. His lips trembled as he kissed the paddle and then held it up for me in a ceremonious manner.

Willie palmed his hands against the floor, hoisted himself to his socked toes and his ass globes and the scent from them were in my face. My God, the sight of those ass globes in that position, the cheeks of them slightly parted, revealing the exotically beautiful guy's velvet highway nearly sent me over the edge. I took a deep breath, raised my paddle high… and brought it crashing down on the guy's ass globes.

WHAPPPP WHAPPPP WHAPPPP WHAPPPP WHAPPPP WHAPPPP WHAPPPP WHAPPPP WHAPPPP WHAPPPP WHAPPPP WHAPPPP

"OOOOOOOOH SIR, SIR," Willie sniveled loudly, the sounds coming from deep in his throat as I again administered to him a good old-fashioned spanking. "YOWWWWWWW…"

As I went on and on and on paddling him, harder and more stinging with each blow, Willie sang out a song of constant outrage and pain as his delectable rear absorbed the blows of my leather paddle.

"OOOOOOOOHHHHH, OWWWWWWWWW," Willie screamed, music to my ears… and cock.

And speaking of cock, despite the pain (and pleasure) I was causing in my handsome spanked Dominican guy, I could feel how hard his cock was as it pressed against my lap, his balls churning, warm and pressing on my lap as well.

I raised my paddle higher and brought it swooping down, HARD…

WHAPPPP WHAPPPP WHAPPPP WHAPPPP WHAPPPP WHAPPPP WHAPPPP

"AAAYYYYYYYYY!!!" Willie ranted, now howling sounds of constant outrage and pain due to the predicament he was in, as his rear no doubt was stinging beyond his comprehension.

He pressed his palms harder against the floor, raised himself up higher over my lap and I simply paddled him harder yet.

AND, after what had to be another good fifty to sixty hard swats on those ass globes of Willie's that I had come to adore, there was definitely an unbelievable burning in them, causing the guy to bounce around like a mad puppet. HA, Willie's mouth, that fucking exquisite mouth that had sucked my cum and his own ass chowder off my fingers was in a constant "O" of outrage as he howled about what I was doing and doing and doing to his ass cheeks. My God, no one ever saw a more magnificent shade of brown mixed with RED, hot red.

A short while later I had Willie standing on his red socked feet, his legs spread shoulder-wide, leaning over, and his palms pressed against the sides of the closed door of the bedroom/playroom we were in. I had tied a black cloth blindfold over the HOT as hell Latin guy's eyes before ordering him into the position he was now positioned at.

Up on your toes Velvet highway," I railed at the guy, caressing his sweet coconut shaped ass cheeks with my leather paddle. Those delectable ass globes of his twitched with a life all their own, pure heaven to witness, and his pink bunghole was then displayed between his brown and red cheeks, OH MAN, even though I had already fucked the guy I knew I was ready for another go round at that as well… as soon as I had spanked and paddled him some more that is.

With that, I raised my leather paddle, swung back a bit and once more brought it crashing down on Willie's butt cheeks.

"YOWWWWWWW!!!! OH SIR, how much can one man's ass take???" Willie cried out pitifully, dancing oh so sexily on his red socked toes.

"Oh my sexy Velvet highway, you would be amazed at just how much abuse one posterior can take," I teased my now blindfolded hot Dominican guy.

He gripped the sides of the doorway tighter, clenched his teeth and his tears soaked his blindfold as I thrashed and whapped and swatted his ass cheeks over and over and over and over, the sound of leather meeting flesh was maddening for the guy and sensuous for me.

WHAPPPP WHAPPPP WHAPPPP WHAPPPP WHAPPPP WHAPPPP WHAPPPP WHAPPPP Went my leather paddle as it connected meanly over and over again on Willie's jutted out ass cheeks. FUCK, I hadn't even tied the guy's hands and he had allowed me to blindfold him, he had instantly positioned himself in the manner that I had ordered him into, he was a TOTAL submissive, totally and erotically beautiful and so able to take what I was dishing out on him. As I had said, Willie had an ass made to be spanked and paddled... and other things as well.

"OHHHHHHHHHH..." Willie cried, sniveled and pouted as I continued paddling him.

The pain in Willie's ass, by then, had to be as if a pot of boiling water had been tossed over it. And also by then, his tears had more than soaked the blindfold I had tied over his eyes; his tears were actually streaming down the sides of his beautiful blindfolded face.

By the time I finally stopped paddling and whapping Willie's delectable ass globes he was broken by sobs and wailing. I had obviously pushed him across the line. I had turned him from a man into a sniveling crybaby. As he howled in pain I dropped my leather paddle to the floor, grabbed Willie around his stomach area, hoisted him off the floor and lowered him down a second time on my throbbing baby maker.

"OOOOOOOO…" Willie crooned in between crying as I literally impaled him on my hard thick manhood.

"YEAH, there ya go, another good workout for your velvet highway Velvet Highway," I rasped at the guy as I lugged him around on my cock, hoisting him up and down on it, the sounds of squishing now filling the sex-filled air.

Because I had already shot a whopper of a load earlier inside Willie's velvet highway, it took me a tad longer to cum the second time around. I sat down on the bed where I had spanked Willie and rode the still blindfolded guy up and down and up and down on my erection.

When I shot my second load inside the HOT Latin guy I grunted and swore like a marine, AND, at the same time Willie grabbed his hard cock and spewed his mess all over his hairless delectable chest. As he creamed and screamed in a man's passion I reached around him and grabbed those pointy as darts tits of his again. He screamed a tad louder and as I squeezed and twisted his tits the guy spewed even more mess all over himself, FUCK YEAH…

After a while my cock shriveled inside Willie's velvet highway and he climbed off me, his own cock spent between his legs as well. As he stood up, still shaking a bit he reached up and lowered the blindfold I had put on him, leaving it dangling around his neck. He turned and faced me, looking down at me as I sat on the bed.

"Thank you Sir, you really know how to treat a guy," Willie whispered, wiping tears from his eyes, but not rubbing the burn from his ass cheeks.

"You're not so bad yourself Velvet Highway," I replied and we smiled at each other. "Well, I suppose we should get back out to the party."

"Yes, I suppose we should, but I doubt that I will participate in the next game of pairing tops with bottoms, I don't think my bottom could take much more," Willie said and we both laughed as we exited the playroom.

The End

Eric's Sandals

Author: Christopher Trevor

Part 1

*Story Inspired by: Eric, a young handsome executive
in sandals on the 6 train during a recent weekend...*

"OOOOOHHHHH..." was the sound Eric Smith made as
he slowly opened his eyes, realizing as he did open them
that his vision was most hazy and blurred, though he did not
know why.

The curly dark haired young finance executive found
to his total shock that he was laying stretched out on his back
atop a long, wide, smooth oak-topped conference room-like
table. But as the handsome young man turned his head from
side to side to try to take in his surroundings he was quickly
able to surmise that this was not a conference room he had
just woken up in...

"What in the... where am I?" Eric whispered as he lay there feeling sluggish and mostly confused, as the room seemed to spin around him.

He tried to collect his thoughts as they spiraled through his mind and with his teeth clenched and his hands at his sides curled into fists in frustration the last thing the well-toned young executive remembered was having been on the number 6 train, returning from a shopping excursion at Bloomingdale's on 59th Street in New York City.

"Y-yeah, I was on the train, minding my own business," Eric said to himself softly. "And then, then... some dude, dude looked like Henry Winkler sat down on my left... and another dude, a black dude, sat down on my right... yeah, I was centered between those two dudes... and..."

and it was when the Henry Winkler dude said that he liked my sandals that the unusual conversations started with these guys who had centered me... and... and... and then I was here... shit... shit, wherever here is..."

Suddenly, as Eric lay there trying to sort out his thoughts he saw two figures stand over him at the sides of the table he was laid out on...

"You okay bud?" someone said, and to Eric it sounded very, very far away, as if the person was speaking through an echo-chamber of some sort.

"Who... who..." Eric asked, realizing that as well as the fact that he was laid out atop some table that all he was wearing was his tight white briefs by Calvin Klein and the sandals he had made himself.

Gone were Eric's beige cargo shorts by The Gap and the pullover light blue zippered polo shirt he had had on, by Ralph Lauren. He squirmed and wiggled himself a bit as he lay there and lifted his head a tad, looking down at himself in his near naked sexy glory. He was not tied up or lashed to the table he was laying on, yet he could not seem to move as he would like to, in other words to get up off the table and get the hell out of wherever he presently was…

"Yeah, he's okay, just a bit out of it," the other figure standing over him said, and again it sounded very, very far away to Eric. "What with the way we dosed him it's no wonder he's so bewildered…"

"WH-where… where…" Eric managed to whimper softly.

"Just relax dude, just relax…" Eric then heard the first figure who had spoken earlier say down at him and then he saw through his blurred vision what looked like some sort of spray can heading toward his face… or, more precisely heading toward his nose and mouth.

"What… what is…?" Eric asked and then he was treated to a face-full of whatever the contents of the spray can were that was pointed at his boyishly handsome face… "UHHHHHHHH…"

Eric inhaled and the scent was rancid and awful… and overpowering… and as his head slid back down to the tabletop and his eyes again closed, sleep claimed the handsome young executive…

As Eric lay there in a most sleepy stupor his head spun and moved back and forth… and as he then felt as if he were somehow floating, was when he felt the delicate kisses, licks and smooches being bestowed on his sandaled feet…

"OOOOOOO… what in the…" Eric whispered, so softly that even the figures at the end of the table at his feet, six of them to be exact, did not hear him. "Whasss goin' on???"

Try as he may he was unable to open his eyes this time... and he simply lay there feeling more and more bewildered, confused... and fear-filled as well...

As whoever they were at his sandaled feet licked, kissed, smooched and ran their tongues over the tops, sides and sandal straps of them Eric again tried to make sense of the last thing he could recall...

"I-I was on the number 6 train, yeah, that's it, the train... and that dude who sat on my left said he liked my sandals... and... and..." Eric mumbled but then once more he was treated to a face-full of the rancid stinking contents of the spray can from a few minutes earlier. "UHHHHHHHHHH..."

As total sleep claimed the young finance executive this time the last thing he heard someone say was, "Damn, he sure is a strong dude... took two doses to knock him out that time..."

As Eric slept fitfully he dreamt of when he was on the number 6 train, he had just been shopping/ browsing in Bloomingdales during a Saturday afternoon in the month of April...

... and being that the weather was unseasonably warm he had dressed that day in cargo shorts, a short sleeved polo shirt and his sandals, the sandals that he had made himself... creative dude that he was...

In his dream Eric saw himself board the number 6 train at 59th Street and he sat down in the center seat that would hold three people. As the train moved out of the 59th Street station Eric settled down to relax for the ride home to his downtown Manhattan studio apartment, his shopping bag with the New York Mets logo on it situated between his muscular legs. Glancing up for a moment he saw a guy who looked like the actor, Henry Winkler, and appeared to be in his middle to upper forties toying with his cell phone… or if Eric didn't know better, the guy was maybe sneaking pictures of his sandaled feet with the camera in his cell phone… or maybe not he thought in a silly manner…

After a couple stops the Henry Winkler guy put his cell phone away and sat down next to Eric on his left, just as a young black guy sat down next to him on his right. Eric didn't think a thing about how he was suddenly centered between two dudes, until the guy on his left said to him, "May I ask where you got those sandals?"

Eric smiled, he had been right, the Henry Winkler guy had been taking pictures of his sandaled feet with his camera-phone, but no big deal really, it was flattering in a way, and it was just his feet with his sandals on after all…

Still smiling in a friendly manner Eric said, "I made them…"

"You made them?" the guy asked. "Wow, they are incredible looking… and so different…"

Eric smiled again and then the black guy on his right mumbled something that sounded like, "… asking him about his sandals…" sounding sarcastic as he said it.

"Yeah, I have heard that before…" Eric said to the guy who had just complimented him on his sandals.

"I'm a writer and a photographer, and I would love to photograph you, mostly your sandals and feet…" the guy said then.

"Wow, you're a writer and a photographer?" the black guy on Eric's right then piped up, leaning over a bit to take in the sight of the guy on Eric's left, as Eric himself was trying to take in what the Henry Winkler guy had just said, photograph him? His sandaled feet mostly???

Then, the two men at Eric's sides were leaning against and across him, speaking to each other; the Henry Winkler dude seemed to be wallowing in rubbing against Eric's short-sleeved shirt, right where his upper arm soft skin was exposed.

"Yeah, I write fiction and I wrote a non-fiction book recently," the Henry Winkler guy said to the black guy… and Eric was feeling somewhat sandwiched in between these two dudes, who both seemed to have designs on him, but for different reasons it would appear to the young finance executive.

"Wow, that is awesome," the black guy said to the Henry Winkler guy as he leaned over Eric. "And you make sandals…"

"Well, I don't make sandals for a living, I work in finance actually," Eric piped up, squirming his arms in closer, a strange feeling engulfing him as the two men seemed to be squeezing him in more-so.

"Ah, finance, so from Monday to Friday you're a suit," the Henry Winkler guy said and Eric turned to look at him head-on. "… all the more reason I would love to photograph you…"

"What uh, what exactly does that mean?" Eric asked a mischievous looking grin on his handsome face. "What does that mean… what does… what…?"

"What does that mean…" Eric whispered now atop the table through quivering lips.

At that point the dream seemed to fade and Eric heard the sound of bells as the train doors opened and closed to let people off and on at the next stop… and as the dream faded he again managed to open his eyes as he lay atop the conference-room table. As he came to this time he realized just how sleek and smooth and cool the tabletop that he was stretched out on really was against his naked back and the backs of his muscular legs...

"OOOOOOOHHHH..." Eric swooned and opened his eyes, once more taking in his blurry and oh so out of focus surroundings.

"WH-what is this place?" Eric whispered and again lifted his head partway up. "Where in the hell am I? Can someone tell me that?"

He pressed his palms flat against the tabletop and looked down at his sandaled feet, those feet and sandals being what seemed to have gotten him into this predicament... or had they??? Was the guy from the train part of the reason he was here now??? And again he had to ask himself, "Where exactly is here???"

Then, as his vision cleared a bit Eric saw six figures standing at the end of the table, over his sandaled feet to be exact. The room he was in seemed to be pretty big with whitewashed looking walls, or was that white his blurred vision? The young finance executive could not be sure. He squinted his eyes a bit and pressing his palms harder against the tabletop he desperately tried to lift his head more off the table, the desire to see who the hell the six people were at the end of the table overpowering him it seemed.

"Who... who..." he muttered, not able to speak normally either and then felt each of his sandaled ankles grabbed in firm strong grips. "What..."

Eric watched as the shadowed figures lifted his sandaled feet upwards and then all six of the figures made their move... sniffing, kissing, licking, smooching and trailing tongues all over his feet in unison...

"OOOOOOOOOO..." Eric moaned and squinted his eyes harder, a look of disbelief on his gloriously handsome face. "What... what are you all doing with my feet??? Please tell me... what... who... oh my word..."

As his feet were literally orally worshipped Eric felt the first stirrings of his cock in his white briefs... but then, from both sides of the table the finance executive saw not one, but two spray cans this time pointed at his nostrils and mouth.

"OH no..." Eric croaked miserably and once more he was sprayed into dreamland it seemed...

His head slid back to the tabletop again, his mouth quivered and Eric Smith slept, and dreamt... and tried to make sense of all of this insanity...

As his tortured mind spun Eric somehow returned to the memory dream of being on the 6 train... with the two dudes, one a Henry Winkler look-a-like and the other a not so bad looking black guy... both of whom seemed to have designs on the boyishly handsome young executive in his casual weekend wear... for different reasons though it seemed...

"What does that mean?" Eric asked the Henry Winkler guy when he had just been told by him that he would love to photograph him.

"Well, like I said, I'm a writer and a photographer," the Henry Winkler guy reiterated for the befuddled Eric. "And mostly what I photograph are men in suits and ties, dress shoes and dress socks... sometimes with their shoes off, just their socked feet..."

"Heh, there you go with my feet again," Eric said and wiggled his naked toes in his handmade sandals.

"One of the pictures I took recently of a model made it onto the cover of my latest book," the Henry Winkler guy said and by that Eric was impressed.

"Wow that is pretty cool, what kind of fiction do you write and what kind of non-fiction do you write?" Eric said.

"Well, my only non-fiction book so far deals with teenage bullying and…" the Henry Winkler guy said.

"Yeah, awesome," Eric said and then to his surprise felt the black guy on his other side grip his arm, right where his shirt sleeve ended.

"That is great dude," the black guy said as the Henry Winkler guy was taking out a business card for Eric. "But you see, I'm an actor… and…"

"That's cool too, an actor and a writer and a photographer," the Henry Winkler guy said as once more he and the black guy were talking across the confused feeling young finance executive, and the black guy was holding his arm now in a steely almost possessive way.

"Man, did you ever think that you would meet both an actor and a guy who was a writer and a photographer in one train sitting dude?" the black guy asked Eric, his eyes seeming to bore into his very being, as he squeezed and rubbed his thumb almost lovingly over Eric's arm in his grip.

"N-no, never would have thunk it dudes," Eric quipped and all three of the men laughed good naturedly.

"Well anyway, this is my stop," the Henry Winkler guy said after handing Eric his business card and getting to his feet. "Please do contact me; you would be a joy to photograph."

"Yeah, uh, sure, I guess…" Eric said, watching as the guy disembarked from the train on 34th Street… and was left with the black guy… who was still holding his arm tight.

"What man?" Eric asked, looking into the black guy's eyes… and then once more he heard the sounds of the train bells as the doors closed and the memory dream faded… and in his fitful sleep state he felt his sandaled feet being licked, smooched, tongued, and kissed by very many pairs of lips as they were held aloft.

"He-he didn't let go of my arm…" Eric mumbled to himself, his lips barely moving as he spoke, his chest slowly inching up and down as he lay atop the table. "… and they-they're not letting go of my ankles…"

He struggled to open his eyes yet again and looked across himself and down at his feet…

What he saw… and felt was beyond his rational belief…

Whoever these people were, six figures standing there, two of them holding his feet aloft by his ankles, were literally worshipping and licking and kissing and smooching and sucking his sandaled feet. The sensations were riveting at that point and then one of the figures worked their mouth over one of his arches as if they were eating corn on the cob.

"OOOOOOOOO GAWD…" Eric groaned and arched his head back, pressing his palms hard again against the tabletop. "Why… why are you all doing this to me???"

In response to his question all six figures at the end of the table doubled the speed at which they were working on the young man's sandaled feet… The sounds of his feet being licked, kissed, smooched and his arches both being eaten now in a corn on the cob style drove the young executive into a tizzy, a total sexual yearning... as his cock was now beyond erect in his white briefs...

"WH-what in all hell goes on here???" Eric blurted, his head still arched back, his chest raised up a bit off the table. "Got to, got to get out of this..."

"Oh no dear sandaled boy, because you see, the fun is just starting after all..." Eric heard someone above his head area say and when he straightened himself out and looked up he was again looking into the nozzle of a spray can.

"AW no, please, whoever you are, don't put me to sleep again huh?" Eric begged. "That stuff stinks..."

"But your feet don't, they're simply delectable and just right," the person with the spray can said... and to Eric's dismay they sprayed him back to dreamland once more...

"UUUUHHHHHHH..." Eric swooned miserably. "B-bastards... UUUUHHHH..."

And once more his handsome head sunk back to the tabletop...

Chapter 2

As Eric slept off the latest dose of whatever it was that whoever it was had sprayed into his mouth and nostrils umpteen times it seemed to the befuddled young executive, he once again found himself in the memory dream of having been on the number 6 train. As his mind drifted back to the dream he fleetingly thought to himself..."Of all the cars and of all the seats on the fucking train to sit in I had to choose the one where I would be spoken to by a guy who looked like Henry Winkler and honed in on my damned sandaled feet... and a black dude who seems to be trying to seduce my handsome ass... why didn't I tell him to let go of my damned arm???"

"By the by my name is Jerome," the black guy said to Eric as the train barreled on through Manhattan, and after the Henry Winkler guy had gotten off and someone else had sat down on Eric's left.

The black guy "finally" let go of Eric's upper arm and held out his hand to shake.

"Nice uh, nice to meet you Jerome, my name is Eric," Eric responded and held out his hand as well.

The two men shook hands and then Jerome said, "So man, that guy really seemed to like your feet huh?"

Smiling and blushing, Eric stretched his sandaled feet out in front of himself, wiggled his toes again and replied, "Yeah, never had someone so gaga over my feet before, but I think it was more my sandals that he liked, I think he even took some pictures of my sandaled feet with his cell phone camera..."

"WOW, that was flattering huh dude?" Jerome asked, grinning in Eric's face.

"Sort of I suppose, stalkerish as well if you ask me," Eric replied.

"And besides working in finance you make your own line of sandals huh?" Jerome asked it not lost on Eric at that point how the guy was looking at him most lustfully at that point.

"Well, no, like I said, I made these, only these," Eric said, glancing down again at his sandaled feet and inwardly wishing he had opted to wear sneakers and sweat socks that day, wondering if that would have helped him to have avoided this strange conversation where his damned feet, of all things were concerned.

"And what was it that made you want to make those sandals Eric?" Jerome asked and hooked his hand AGAIN around the handsome young executive's arm.

"Well, being in finance I know just how bad the economy is nowadays," Eric said and gulped hard and silently as Jerome squeezed his arm tighter yet, inflicting just a bit of pain, but Eric didn't say boo about it, for whatever the fuck the reason. "... and men's leather sandals can be uh, really expensive, especially for a dude like me... who uh, wants to live in Manhattan... you understand..."

"I think I do Eric, I think I do..." Jerome said, leaning in closer to the bewildered Eric and holding tighter still to his upper arm. "So tell me more about those sandals of yours and how you made them... dude..."

"Well, uh, what can I say, I've always liked sandals," Eric said. "But I wanted a pair that stood out somehow, that was totally me, you know? But anyway...

men's leather sandals, like all leather shoe wear for men, are very expensive. It makes much more sense to try to create your own home-styled, fashionable leather sandals.

Now you may think this is next to impossible, but obviously I did it, and I did some research and found out that centuries ago, that's exactly what was done, and they never had the modern tools and conveniences we enjoy today. Making men's leather sandals may sound difficult, but is a fun and fulfilling project to do."

"And how long did it take you to make those babies on your feet?" Jerome asked, this time holding even tighter to Eric's upper arm after having gripped it.

"Well uh, not long," Eric replied, glancing at Jerome's hand as it circled his upper arm just above his shirt sleeve and then looked into the black guy's leering and hunger-filled eyes. "Yeah… uh, not long…"

"What was the process?" Jerome asked.

Well, once you've have mastered the art of forming sandals, you can experiment with style and design, that's how I started before I finally completed these, it was a lot of hit and miss you see," Eric explained, feeling a bit more than odd as the black guy held onto his arm almost for dear life it seemed. "You can work with different colors or shades, and even make women's sandals for someone special, if uh, you know what I mean?"

"I think I do bud, I think I do," Jerome replied with an evil looking grin.

"You uh, do like women I take it huh Jerome?" Eric asked and again glanced at the black guy's hand circled about his upper arm.

"Sure do, so tell me more about how you made those sandals you got on," Jerome replied, breathing heavily into Eric's handsome face as he said it and kneaded his arm now. "What would you tell an actor who may want to make a pair of sandals for a part he would have to play say in a TV show or maybe even the big, big time… a movie…"

"Well, okay, I suppose that's good a reason as any for a guy to want to make his own sandals," Eric replied, now watching the stops on the train, thanking his lucky stars that his stop was coming up soon. "Make an outline of your feet. Do one for each foot because often, there's a slight difference in the length of your feet. Use cork tiles. Then after that cut out the outlines, but leave an allowance of about an inch and a half on all sides. Use a sharp cutter. Once done with that, cut an outline once more, but use plywood instead. After that, you want to glue both outlines together using super glue or a hot glue gun. Check that you glue the left outlines together, and right foot outlines together as well."

"I'm with you man, I'm with you," Jerome said. "WOW, the way you're describing making those awesome looking sandals you got on makes me think that that Henry Winkler look-a-like guy should have stayed on the train with us huh Eric?"

"Yeah, maybe he should have…" Eric said and then to himself he said, "Or maybe not…"

Eric swallowed hard as Jerome held tighter and tighter to his upper arm, and instead of causing a scene on a crowded train and asking the guy to let go of him he rambled on instead with his instructions for making men's sandals…

"Okay, to get on with it, cut two leather pieces, 3 by 7 inches, no more, no less," Eric went on. "These will serve as the sandal heel section."

"NICE," Jerome said. "Real nice Eric…"

At that point Eric gulped visibly and looked directly into Jerome's eyes…

"Say bud, could you uh loosen up on me here?" Eric asked, indicating with his eyes Jerome's hand as it was squeezing his arm to the point now that it felt like an overly tight blood pressure cuff on it. "I appreciate that you might uh, like me and all, but you're hurting me…"

Shit, sorry Eric, would never want to hurt you dude," Jerome chuckled and let go of the young executive's arm.

"Thanks man," Eric said, breathing a sigh of relief. "Anyway, I get off in a couple of stops so let me quickly finish telling you how to make sandals like the ones I got on, huh?"

"Sure thing bud, sure thing," Jerome said. "Damn, didn't mean to hurt you Eric, I'm just real friendly you know?"

"Yeah, sure, I can tell," Eric said with a half a smile on his handsome face.

"Okay, cut four pieces of 2 by 5 inch pieces of leather for the sides of your sandals," Eric continued, a strange feeling engulfing him then as he spoke, the strange feeling in his cock... of all places... DAMN. "Measure them up against your base outline, and trim them if necessary. Trim scallop edges along the top of the side pieces. Be sure not to cut to the bottom of the sides. You can also start adding some designs like crescent moon shapes, stars or simple holes around the sides of your sandals. This is where your creativity will show, I know it's where mine showed, and I opted for strap-ups on my sandals, as you can see. You can glue the shapes or cut through the leather. These shapes, if you cut them out, should be small enough to fit the laces. You will need them to bring the sandals together. Then, staple your heel leather pieces to your sandal soles. Cut small lace holes as well so you can lace up from back to front. Next, staple your heel leather pieces to your sandal outer soles, the wood side should be up. Cut small laces holes on the leather heel pieces and then begin to lace up from back to front."

"Damn, you make it sound so easy Eric," Jerome exclaimed.

"It really is, once you get the hang of it," Eric said.

"Yeah, the hang of it, that sounds like a good idea," Jerome laughed.

"Huh?" Eric asked.

"Nothing, nothing, sorry I interrupted you bud, go on, please go on," Jerome said.

"Okay, anyway, staple your leather sides to the soles and lace your sandals through the holes you cut. The laces are essentially what will keep all pieces together and form the sandals. Polish and wax your leather sandals periodically to maintain the softness of the leather, and prevent cracks… and that's it, you got your own homemade sandals…" Eric said in conclusion.

"WOW, that is so awesome," Jerome said, his pearly white teeth showing almost in fang-like fashion.

"Anyway man, this is my stop," Eric said, reaching down for his shopping bag with the Mets baseball team logo on it. "It was really nice meeting you and talking with you."

"Same here Eric, same here," Jerome said, holding out his hand once more.

Being the gentleman that he was Eric shook hands with Jerome and as he did he felt a slight pinch in the palm of his hand.

"WH…" Eric began but was unable to complete the word as Jerome then once more gripped Eric's upper arm as well… and again the young finance executive felt a pinch, this one more pronounced than the one in his hand. "WH…"

Suddenly, Eric slumped back into his seat and let go of the handles of his shopping bag.

"Hey buddy, you okay?" Jerome asked, saying it loud enough for everyone within earshot to hear.

"I-I feel funny…" Eric said and when he looked around everything appeared to be blurry and out of focus. "WH-what did you…"

But before Eric could finish asking his question Jerome quickly gripped the guy's upper arm again, and Eric felt a third pinch…

"Oh holy shit..." Eric whispered and as his eyes closed he knew he was in some sort of trouble... REAL TROUBLE...

From somewhere far away it seemed then, Eric heard someone say to Jerome, "Hey man, is your friend okay there?" and then Jerome replying, "I think so, maybe the train was too crowded for him and he became faint, not enough air. Could you maybe help me carry him up to the street? Get him some air, that should help him I think... I'm a paramedic after all..."

"Damn, lucky for him," the other voice said.

In his stupor Eric wanted to say that the guy was not a paramedic, that he was an actor... wasn't he???

"Okay, you support his upper body against you and I'll hold his feet as we go up the stairs," Eric heard the other voice say and then he was hoisted between the two men and lugged out of the subway car and onto the station, amid the stares of non-caring passengers who moved out of their way, those passengers who only wanted to be on their way as soon as possible.

This was New York after all...

As he was carried between the two men Eric felt the guy holding his feet caressing his sandal straps...

"Damn, these sure are nice sandals he's got on," Eric heard the other voice say as the two men were then lugging him up the stairs, out of the subway station, onto a crowded New York street... and finally depositing the young finance executive in the back seat of a large black stretch limousine...

As the door slammed shut and Eric fell deeper into a sleepy stupor he heard Jerome say, "That'll be fifty thousand dollars bud..."

As Eric came to once more atop the table he muttered to himself, "Shit, holy fucking shit, I was kidnapped... I was literally fucking kidnapped... and right off a crowded New York City subway train at that..."

As he swooned and squirmed again on the tabletop Eric suddenly, again, felt hyper sensations at his feet.

"UHHHHHHHH... WH-What now???" the young finance executive muttered and cautiously lifted his head, wary at this point of the fact that he would more than likely be gassed back to dreamland yet again.

But as he looked across himself this time through blurred vision Eric took in the fact that his two big toes were being SAVAGELY sucked on, his now naked feet being gripped TIGHT by whoever the two figures were that were leaning down over his feet and sucking his big toes like they were cocks.

"OOOOOOO... OOOOOOHHH my word," Eric crooned and managed to lift his head a tad higher.

He saw that his prized sandals, they being what had seemed to have gotten him into this mess in the first place were no longer on his feet, rather they were set on the table a few inches away from his now naked feet...

...his now naked feet whereon his big toes were being sucked by what appeared to be two men... and while his big toes were in their mouths he felt their tongues caressing and swirling over his well-pedicured toenails... and as they caressed his toenails with their tongues they gripped his naked feet tighter and tighter, digging their thumbs especially into the meaty bottoms of his soles...

Eric's feet were literally tingling and alive and he was astonished to realize that he felt it in his erect cock as it pounded thick and hard in his white briefs, the only clothing he still had on at that point.

"Oh but this is unreal…" the young finance executive stated and managed to sit up a tad more at that point, his vision still blurred and fuzzy though.

But then, a thin leather riding-crop was suddenly pressed against his upper chest and just under his nipples.

"Huh?" Eric asked and looked down at the device as it was pressed against him, teasing his nipples just a bit.

The riding-crop was pressed harder against his chest and Eric found himself being propelled back onto his back atop the table.

"P-please don't put me to sleep again, please," Eric mumbled miserably and with a feeling of forced ecstasy coursing through his entire well-toned body at that point. "C-could you maybe tell me what this is all about…"

Unable to resist Eric simply laid back atop the smooth surface of the table and breathed heavily, causing his muscular chest to heave up and down a bit as he pressed his palms again flat against the table.

"I think perhaps you've had enough for now sandaled boy," Eric heard the voice over him saying as the riding-crop was slid lecherously across his nipples and off his chest. "… enough to keep you as docile as we want that is…"

"D-docile?" Eric asked as his two big toes were again being crazily and hungrily sucked on. "Man, I'm feeling anything but docile bud… I'm feeling really confused at the moment… and scared shit-less to say it plainly…"

As the person stood on Eric's right side at his chest out of the corner of his eye Eric saw another figure step to his left side, also at his chest. The figure on his right trailed the tip of the riding-crop over Eric's beefy pink nipples, teasing them, causing them to jut up like two pencil erasers.

"H-hey, first my feet, then my toes, and now my danged nips of all things?" Eric moaned and clenched his teeth.

"I love it, he calls them his danged nips..." the figure on Eric's left laughed, sounding sort of deranged.

Then, to Eric's total shock the two figures at his chest leaned down and slurped one of his jutted up nipples each into their mouths.

"UUUUUUHHHHHH..." Eric gasped. "Oh holy shit you guys..."

The young finance executive clenched not only his teeth this time but his hands into fists as his two big toes were sucked and now his nipples.

"Oh damn, oh fuck..." Eric muttered and as he was feasted on at the toes and nipples his head spun away and his cock churned thick and beefy and hard in his white briefs. "What in all hell IS THIS about???"

The sounds of sucking, slurping, smooching and licking filled the air around Eric and he squeezed his eyes shut... as a feeling of erotic humiliation filled him... for he suddenly shot a whopper of a load right into his white briefs, moaning and grunting in a man's passion as he came... thrashing atop the table, shivering, and then passed out on his own this time...

Chapter 3

A while later, Eric had no idea really how much later though, the young finance executive climbed wearily back to consciousness yet again…

"WWWUUUUHHH…" he groaned and cocked his head back… and realized that because he was able to cock his head back and it hit only empty air, that he was no longer stretched out atop the table he had been lying on. "I-I shot my goddamned load… I shot my load from having my damned toes and nipples sucked on, oh holy shit and humiliation…"

As his vision somewhat adjusted Eric looked around and realized to his dismay that he was still in a shitload of trouble… because this time he was fastened by thick bungee rope that had been secured under his arms along with a sturdy leather harness around his chest area that extended downward and was strapped around his waist area… and he was dangling a few feet off the floor in what he was able to determine was a gym of some sort.

"AW holy shit on a shingle, what now?" Eric exclaimed miserably as his vision finally, FINALLY, began to clear up…

The young finance executive twisted and jostled himself a bit in his bindings, squirming miserably when he came to the realization that his wrists were restrained in leather cuffs at his sides and that the leather cuffs were connected to the harness area around his waist.

"Damn, this time they, whoever the fucks THEY are really got me in a bind," Eric blabbered angrily.

Looking down at the floor Eric saw his sandals there; mere inches away from where he had been hung up....and to further his dismay, next to his sandals were the young finance executive's white briefs.

"Shit, my sandals... they took my sandals off me... fuck, never thought a pair of leather sandals would cause me so much grief... OR get me kidnapped... AND MY BRIEFS... Holy crap..." Eric shrilled. "Now I'm fucking naked as the day I was born..."

Looking down some more Eric studied his briefs and noted the globs and thick remnants of his cum in them.

"Damn, never shot so much... and just from having my damned feet worked over, of all things..." Eric muttered miserably.

From the way his sandals and briefs were set up next to each other under where he dangled Eric somehow got the feeling that the last of his clothing items had not just been tossed there, no, the way they were situated was like some sort of a shrine... but a shrine to what the young finance executive wondered miserably.

From behind him Eric felt fingertips suddenly trailing down his naked succulent looking ass cheeks.

"WHHHH..." Eric panted at the sensual touch and tried to crane his head around to see who it was being so brazen and taking such fucked up liberties with him.

"Getting the hang of things at this point sandal boy?" a voice asked Eric and then trailed fingers down the outside of his ass crack, sending chills down Eric's spine.

"Yeah fucker, I'm getting the goddamned hang of it, literally it would seem like now." Eric responded. "When in all hell is this going to stop? When are you going to tell me what goes on here huh???"

"A smart dude like you, and you haven't figured it out yet?" the voice behind him asked Eric and whoever they were continued trailing their fingertips up and down against the young finance executive's ass crack.

"WHHHHHHH... p-please man, please don't do that," Eric panted and in response the person behind him simply chuckled and then to further Eric's astonishment they jammed two thick fingers deep into his anal hole. "YUUUUHHH... hey dude, that's my shit chute you're canoodling back there..."

While whoever it was behind him dug deeper into Eric's anal canal the young finance executive suddenly found himself being hoisted higher in his bungee rope and harness prison.

"H-hey, what gives?" Eric panted, swinging his feet around like crazy as up he went... until his naked feet would be aligned with the face of anyone who would be standing in front of him. "Let me down dudes..."

As Eric looked around through still blurred vision he saw two OVERLY MUSCULAR guys at his sides, who were the two hoisting and yanking on the ropes connected to him.

"UHHHHHH..." Eric panted as they secured the slack of the ropes they were holding to sturdy wall hooks, thus jamming Eric in place. The person behind Eric extracted their fingers slowly from his anal opening and then stepped in front of him, looking upward at the prize they had acquired.

"So beautifully handsome," the person whispered and reached into their pants pocket.

Looking downward through his blurred hazy vision Eric tried to make out the person's features and said, "So glad you approve of my looks dude... and..."

But then, to Eric's dismay he saw that what the person had extracted from their pocket was a spray can.

"AW no, no, not that shit again... please dude..." Eric pleaded as the person reached upward, pointing the nozzle of the spray can at Eric's face.

Ignoring the captured and befuddled young finance executive the person pushed down on the plunger, treating poor Eric to a face-full of the rancid smelling fumes.

"YUUUUUUHHHH..." Eric grunted and his head fell back and dangled. "A-a smart dude like me???"

As he slid into a stupor yet again Eric heard the sounds of evil laughter below him. As he managed to look down a bit through what appeared to be thick clouds of sleep he could see once again six figures there, and this time they were gathered at his dangling, naked feet. One of the six figures gripped Eric's right foot at the center and held tight as another of them grabbed his left foot and held it the same way.

"UHHHHHHH..." Eric groaned in a lusty manner as he felt his feet being squeezed and kneaded. "WHHH..."

"Such delectable feet he has," the person holding Eric's right foot exclaimed.

"I couldn't agree more," the person with Eric's left foot in hand said.

As the two figures standing in front of Eric held his feet tight and squeezed them like they were lemons being used to make lemonade two more of the figures took position behind the dangling young finance executive.

As the two figures holding Eric's feet tight pulled them forward a bit and began slurping at not just his big toes this time, but each toe alternately, driving the stupored young man into a new tizzy, Eric felt fingertips trailing up and down and in circular motions around the backs of his heels.

"AWWWWWWHHHH..." Eric hemmed and managed to thrash his head forward so that now it was dangling down in front of him.

"You think we should have blindfolded him?" Eric heard someone ask.

"Nah, the way I dosed him he won't be able to see straight for some time," came the response and Eric's heart sunk. "No way will he ever be able to figure out who we are..."

Then, Eric felt his cock churning and beginning to stiffen again as his toes were alternately sucked, his feet were squeezed and kneaded and the backs of his heels were not just being fingered... but at that point they were being kissed and licked and smooched as well...

"OOOOOOOOOO..." Eric swooned, trying to make sense of all of this.

"D-dudes, dudes sure do love my damned feet..." Eric said to himself and panted and gasped as he dangled.

Lastly, Eric saw two more figures make their way to the sides of his naked feet...

Watching as best he could through shattered vision and fighting off the effects of whatever the fuck they had continuously dosed him with Eric saw the two figures lean down and begin licking and slathering their tongues over and over and over the tops of his feet.

"OOOOOOOO…" Eric crooned and swooned as six shadowed figures literally feasted on his naked feet, toes, heels and feet-tops.

The two figures licking the tops of his feet drooled over them and licked up their saliva, sending chills through Eric's being and cock…

The two figures behind him pressed their lips against the backs of Eric's heels, kissed and sucked at them and drove him further into a sexual tizzy and the two figures at Eric's toes were now sucking his pinky digits, causing a feeling to course through the young man that he had never experienced before in his young life… as he felt in his cock a tingling that was being caused by what was being done and done and done to his naked feet…

Trying his damndest to climb out of the stupor he had been sprayed into yet again Eric clenched his teeth and looked down at his cock. As he hung there like a slab of beef in a butcher's freezer Eric was humiliated once more to see (through blurred vision that is) that his cock was engorged to the point of erection. He nearly lost it when he felt fingers trailing against his sac and squeezing his balls…

"OHHHHH leave my family jewels alone huh dudes?" Eric panted and gasped madly, not believing what was about to happen yet again. "FUUUCCKKK, I'm shooting my damned load… again…"

The young finance executive thrashed and squirmed in his dangling tied up position as he spewed and shot his load all over his stomach regions.

"AAARRHHHHH, bastards, working my damned feet really seems to set me in motion," Eric swooned, his head spun and like earlier, passed out totally.

Epilogue

"Hey, you okay Sir? Can you hear me? Are you okay?" was the next thing Eric heard as he came to, a deep voice and the feeling of someone holding his chin and rocking his head back and forth.

Eric opened his eyes and saw that he was looking up at two police officers, one who had deep blue eyes, a military style haircut and appeared to be at least six feet tall, give or take an inch. The other police officer, shorter than his partner, had brown eyes and short brown wavy hair.

"WH-what happened?" Eric asked as he looked around and to his TOTAL shock and amazement he was sitting on a bench on the subway station where he had been waiting for the 6 Train earlier, after his window shopping expedition at Bloomingdales. "Officers, I-I was kidnapped... I was..."

Glancing down between his legs Eric saw his shopping bag with the Mets logo on it.

"Kidnapped Sir?" the police officer with the military haircut asked him.

"Y-yes, they, it was a guy who looked like Henry Winkler and a black guy who was an actor and they sat with me on the train and the next thing I knew they were asking about my sandals..."

At that Eric and the two cops looked down at his feet.

"Holy shit," Eric exclaimed when he saw that he was wearing not the sandals he had made himself but a pair of blue Nike sneakers with ankle length white sweat socks, also by Nike. "Shit, where are my sandals?"

"Your sandals Sir?" the shorter cop asked Eric.

"YES, my sandals, what happened to them? When I left the apartment earlier today I was not wearing sneakers and sweat socks and..." Eric railed. "Oh my God, what happened?"

"We found you here sprawled out on the bench Sir, fast asleep, it looked like you had passed out," the first cop said.

"YES, yes, that's it, asleep, I was asleep because they used canned knockout gas on me, repeatedly, I was kidnapped, they knocked me out and they stole my sandals as well, and..." Eric went on and on and then lowered his voice. "And then I shot my load, two times... they were playing with my damned feet and I shot my load..."

"Sir would you like to come to the station and make a statement?" the second cop asked Eric, both of the officers looking at the young finance executive in disbelief.

As Eric looked up at the two cops he realized how bizarre he sounded.

"No, uh, more than likely I did fall asleep here," Eric said. "Probably I dreamt it all..."

"Very good Sir, now the train should be arriving any minute," the first cop said. "If you require any further assistance..."

"No, no, I'll be fine, thanks Officers," Eric said softly and then watched as the two cops walked off and down the station. "But, my sandals..."

Once more Eric looked down at his feet and whispered, "I know I put my sandals on this morning, not sneakers and sweat socks... and fuck, I was on the train already, I was kidnapped. How did I get back here???"

As the train then barreled into the station Eric looked at his watch and his jaw dropped…

As he got to his feet to board the train the two cops watched him from a few feet away on the platform, each of them fingering one of Eric's sandals in the deep pockets of their uniform pants…

A Real Mess

Author: Christopher Trevor

It was Sunday morning, and Jack Rivers and George Cann, two sleazy guys who shared an apartment they rented were sitting in the kitchen just finishing up breakfast while skimming the newspapers.

"What do you feel like doing today man?" Jack asked his buddy, both of them having a day off from their blue collar jobs and nothing to do with it.

"I don't know man, but I'll tell you, I know WHO I'd like to do," George replied, a sneer on his face mixed with a look of total lust in his eyes.

"HA, I don't need three guesses to know that you're talking about that scrungy construction worker in the building across from us, right man?" Jack asked in reply, grabbing and rubbing his crotch as he said it.

"You know it Jacky boy, FUCK, I wasn't going to tell you man, but after you went to sleep last night I watched him and his bitch wife go at it. Man, he fucked her like crazy." George said.

"They didn't see you did they?" Jack asked.

"Nah, they have no fucking idea that our bedrooms face each other across the street," George said. "They're fucking oblivious; too into each other to know we're spying and eyeing them. He has a fucking body like iron, not to mention his cock is of the gargantuan sexy size. I swear jack, I would do ANY fucking thing to get my paws on him."

"Yeah, me too, sad that he has that wife of his there with him," Jack added. "I swear man; if he were all alone we could pay ol' Scrungy a surprise visit."

The two men looked at each other and George said in a lusty tone of voice, "Yeah, if only…"

"I'm going to take a peek at their bedroom," Jack piped up. "Maybe I'll get an eyeful. You never know right? I mean, it's Sunday, and maybe like us, Scrungy and his wife got nothing to do, so maybe they're fucking…"

"Yeah, I think I'll join you," George said.

The two men, clad in jeans, sneakers and tee shirts walked to their bedroom and peered through the thin blinds on the window. What they saw amazed and titillated them, for the construction worker they had nicknamed "Scrungy" and his wife were engaged in an erotic sex play.

"HOOOOLLY shit!" George blurted. "Check that out!"

"Yeah, fuck yeah, Scrungy likes it kinky," Jack said, as what the two sleazy men saw were the big burly construction worker standing with his hands cuffed behind him, a white cloth blindfold tied over his eyes, and his beautiful sexy wife was kneeling in front of him sucking his HUGE cock and fondling his low hanging, size of kiwis balls.

The construction worker, whose name was actually Andy Bowler, towered all of six feet over his wife, he had salt and pepper colored hair, huge muscular arms, and long well-toned tree-trunk like legs. The two sleazy men peered more through the blinds and took in the sight of Andy Bowler's muscular rock-hard-god-like body which was covered in a thick forest of hair, mostly on his chest and legs. George and Jack watched intently, not able to pry themselves away, as the construction worker, clad in only a pair of scuffed up, calf length, black construction worker's boots and white sweat socks tucked down into those boots, was slowly and methodically sucked off by his wife.

"Shit, look at the size of his rod!!" George grunted breathlessly.

"Fuck yeah and fucking A but would I love to wrap my mouth around that," Jack agreed.

"We *have to* nail that fucking guy!" George added. "He has an ass that looks like it's made to be fucked!"

"Damn, if he ever found out we were watching this he would shit a brick and then some," Jack said.

"Or worse man, or worse," George said and snickered.

The two men continued watching... the couple across from their window totally unaware that they were being spied upon.

In the other apartment Samantha Bowler was teasing her hunk of a handcuffed and blindfolded husband as she led him oh so slowly toward orgasm.

"Enjoying this Andy?" the blond haired curvy woman asked her delicious husband.

"AW shit baby, you need to ask?" Andy Bowler replied breathlessly, gasping huskily. "Suck my dick baby; suck my goddamned dick, oh yeah, yeah!"

Samantha sucked her husband some more, squeezing his balls at the same time.

"Oh God baby, you are driving me insane here," the construction worker moaned in a man's passion.

Samantha then moved her tongue down to Andy's big balls and licked them hard, relishing the taste of their mustiness as she did so, running her hands up and down his muscular legs at the same time.

"OHHHHHH... how about taking this blindfold off me now so I can watch?" Andy asked. "You can keep my hands cuffed, no worries there baby..."

"No way, your being blindfolded enhances the fun," Samantha teased and slurped her husband's giant cock back into her mouth, getting a grunt of man's passion out of her colossal husband.

The god-like construction worker struggled not to shoot his load, but then, moments later, he felt his juices about to flow as his sex-crazed wife took him down, down into her throat.

"OH GAWD, oh GOD, oh fuck yeah baby, fuck yeah," Andy shrilled through clenched teeth as his wife swallowed every drop of his offering, him thrusting into her mouth at that point real sexily on his booted feet.

"MMMMMMM..." Samantha crooned around her husband's cock as it spurted and spewed down her throat.

When Andy was spent Samantha stood up and ran her hands all over his rock-hard body, touching and squeezing him everywhere. When she removed her husband's blindfold Andy's bright blue eyes lit up and she kissed him hungrily on the mouth, making him taste his own cum from her lips.

"MMMM... take the cuffs off me, NOW!" the construction worker demanded.

Samantha quickly released her husband and they both flopped down onto the bed together, Andy on top of her. As the still well-horned construction worker prepared to enter his wife, Jack and George were still watching... in awe... from across the way.

"Did you see that???" George asked crazily. "He must have shot a quart of jazz down her throat!"

"Yeah, and now he's going to fuck the bitch!" Jack said just as crazily. "Fuck, he's like a twenty-four hour a day sex machine."

"DAMN, we HAVE TO find a way to land that fucking guy!" George said and then he and Jack watched some more, as Andy's perfectly round and coconuts shaped ass bobbed up and down on the bed...

Sunday Afternoon... and Andy and Samantha Bowler were now sitting in a neighborhood café, enjoying lunch.

"Are you sure you'll be okay for a week while I'm gone to Chicago on my business trip?" Samantha asked her husband after swallowing a mouthful of salad.

"Yes and no," Andy replied with a grin. "I'll of course miss you like crazy, but I'll probably go stir-crazy all by myself, but will I be okay? Sure, I'm a capable man; I can take care of myself.

"It's too bad your company doesn't have any work right now," Andy's wife said. "That would keep you busy."

"Week after next babe," Andy said and took a hearty bight of his hamburger.

"Okay, I'll pack when we get back after brunch, and then I'll call for a cab," Samantha said.

"What time is your flight again?" Andy asked his wife.

"Six PM," Samantha replied, looking at her watch. "And if I'm going to make it we'd better get moving."

The couple ate their food as two men at a nearby table were listening to every word of their conversation. Jack and George smiled triumphantly at each other. Later, back at their apartment, the two men plotted…

"FUCK, I cannot believe how lucky we got!" Jack exclaimed.

"Me either," George agreed. "Scrungy's wife is going to be gone for an entire week!! That construction dude from Heaven is ours man, OURS!!!"

Sunday afternoon, it was five PM and jack and George were watching from their window as Samantha Bowler climbed into a taxi. Her husband, Andy, dressed in navy blue cotton pants by Dickie, a matching tee shirt, black scuffed up construction boots, and white sweat socks, leaned in the window of the cab and kissed his wife goodbye, totally unaware of his impending fate.

"I'll see you in a week," Samantha said softly.

"I love you," Andy said.

"Me too," Samantha replied as Andy then stepped away from the cab.

The construction worker waved at the cab until it was totally out of sight. He then walked back into the apartment building, oblivious of the two men who were watching him from above.

"Let's go," George said breathlessly.

Ten minutes later Andy was back in his apartment, sitting on the couch, drinking a beer, and watching a ball game, when he heard a knock on the door.

"Now who the hell can that be?" the construction worker asked himself as he got to his feet and walked to the door.

"Yah, who's there?" Andy called out loudly and brusquely.

"It's your wife's cab driver Sir," a male voice called out from behind the door. "She says she forgot her purse and asked me to come and get it for her."

Without thinking Andy said, "Oh," opened the door and saw George and Jack standing there.

"Hey, you're not the cab driver," Andy said, feeling confused. "Who are you guys?"

Before the well-muscled construction worker could react, George reached forward, grabbed a handful of Andy's blue tee shirt and yanked the guy forward, tottering him on his booted feet. "YUUUFFFFF!!! H-HEY!!!"

George held Andy and delivered a full-loaded punch to the side of the man's head.

"UNNNGGHHHHH!!!" Andy grunted and fell forward, totally dazed.

And as he fell forward, George quickly slung the burly man over one of his big shoulders.

"Let's get the fuck inside, Scrungy is about to have some unexpected fun."

The two men walked into Andy's apartment. Jack did the honors of locking the door behind them as George shouted, "To the bedroom!" and lumbered with Andy over his shoulder, as Jack followed behind with a backpack.

"WH-what's going on???" Andy muttered as his head spun.

Once they were in the bedroom George set Andy down on wobbly feet and grabbed a handful of his tee shirt again, using it to pull Andy close to him.

"You are in for some real fun Scrungy my man!" George said as Jack put down the backpack and found the handcuffs and the key for them on Samantha's night table.

Leering meanly George held the up the handcuffs for George to see.

"Hey George, look what the fuck I found," Jack laughed.

Smiling evilly George said, "Cuff him now!"

Andy's vision cleared and he turned around to see Jack approaching with the handcuffs.

"HOLY FUCKING shits on a shingle, you two are faggots!! NO!!!!" Andy shouted and tried to pull away from George, but the guy punched him hard again on the side of his head. "UUUHHHNNFFFF!!!"

Andy nearly fell to the floor, but George held him up on his wobbly teetering feet, again using the construction worker's tee shirt as a makeshift handle of sorts.

"You see Jack? The bigger they are, the harder they fall," George mused meanly.

"It's so true man, it's so fucking true," Jack agreed, yanked Andy's wrists behind him and locked them in the handcuffs.

"OHHHH, you, you bastards," Andy muttered as he still wobbled on his booted feet.

"Looking for a third punch Scrungy?" George asked the construction worker. "Trust me on this bud; the next one will put you out for sure."

"S-Scrungy?" Andy asked. "Fuck, what do you guys want, money?"

As he spoke Andy felt Jack's hands roaming down his muscular arms as George yanked him to his tiptoes by his tee shirt.

"Money?" George seethed in Andy's face. "We don't want your money!"

"TH-then what?" Andy asked feeling totally bewildered as to why these two men had muscled their way into his apartment and taken him prisoner.

"Just you Scrungy, just you," George said mockingly and clamped his mouth down on the construction workers and sucked his tongue into his own mouth.

"RRRRRRNNNNN!!!!" Andy screamed as he was for the first time in his life kissed by another guy.

"Oh yeah, kiss him, kiss him the kiss of death," Jack laughed and Andy felt as if he had no choice but to respond to his captor's harsh kiss.

Andy felt George slobbering all over his mouth and grunted "RRRRRMMMGGFFFF!"

When the kiss ended George grabbed Andy's arms and turned him around, facing Jack.

"Your turn Jack," George said and his buddy hooked his hands around Andy's big burly neck.

"C'mon Scrungy boy, let me suck that tongue of yours," Jack said and then, just as George had done, clamped his mouth over the construction workers and sucked his tongue forcefully into his mouth.

"RRRRRRR!!!!" Andy bellowed.

Jack ran his hands through Andy's salt and pepper hair as he sucked his tongue and even kissed his lips. From behind the cuffed construction worker, George squeezed Andy's round tight buns a few times.

Moments later Andy found himself standing helplessly before his two captors…

"What the fuck do you guys want from me???" Andy thundered. "I'm not gay! You two have captured the wrong guy!!

"On the contrary my friend, we have the right fucking guy!" George said. "Because you see, we've been watching you for some time now."

"WATCHING ME???" Andy gasped.

George then took Andy by his arm and walked the handcuffed construction worker over to the bedroom window. Holding Andy's arm in a tight grip he opened the window shade.

"That is our apartment directly across from yours," George explained. "I guess you and your wife never thought that when you left your shade up that anyone was watching you two go at it huh? We'll, we've watched you and your wife on many occasions. And, I must say that we are both quite taken by *you* Scrungy!"

As George spoke he squeezed Andy's arm tighter and spoke directly into the man's ear, his lips grazing the construction worker's earlobe.

"And now you've been taken by us," George snickered and pecked the captive on his cheek.

"*Shit…*" was all Andy was able to mutter as George closed the shade.

"WH-why do you guys call me Scrungy?" Andy asked. "That's not my name, my name is Andy."

"Because big guy, that is what you are, you're scrungy and mean and tough guy looking," George said and let go of Andy's arm. "And now Scrungy, its tittie torture time for you."

With that and in a fast motion George ripped and shredded Andy's shirt off him. He and Jack propped the hapless construction worker against a wall and went to work torturing his pointy, fleshy brown nipples. The two men each slurped one of Andy's big nipples into their mouths, they bit and nipped one of his nipples each, squeezing and slapping his pecs at the same time, inflicting erotic and real pain on the poor guy.

"OWWWCCHHHH!!!! Oh you sick fucks, stop this shit!!!" Andy demanded. "Stop it now!!!"

But Andy's pleas went totally ignored as the two men passionately and hungrily worked his nipples. In minutes the construction worker's man-tits were red, swollen and painfully erect. Jack and George stopped sucking on them and began squeezing, twisting and manhandling them.

"AAARRRRHHHHH…" Andy grunted miserably.

"Okay Jack, I think these tits of his are raw enough now for the tit clamps," George said and Andy's jaw dropped.

"Tit clamps?" Andy whispered in disbelief.

The helpless construction worker watched as Jack opened his backpack and took out a pair of metal, sharp-teethed tit clamps as George was rubbing his thumbs over Andy's nipples, massaging them, teasing them.

"Scrungy, by the time tonight is over you'll be begging us to torture you," George mocked their captive. "You'll come over to our apartment looking for it! Trust me on that, you'll even leave your wife."

"AW, no way man," Andy replied and then saw Jack squeeze the tit clamps open. "Oh shit…"

"Now hold still Scrungy," Jack said and he meanly clipped the tit clamps onto Andy's swollen nipples, TIGHTLY.

"YOWWWWWW!!!" Andy screamed in a man's pain. "Take them off man!! FUCK, take them off!"

"Looks like Scrungy wants to be naked, he wants them off," George laughed.

"NO, NO, not my goddamned clothes you sick fucks…" Andy bellowed.

The two men pulled Andy roughly away from the wall, and together they ripped, stripped and tore the construction worker's blue cotton pants off him.

Poor Andy was left wearing his black scuffed up construction boots, his white sweat socks tucked down into those boots, and a pair of piss stained white Fruit of The Loom briefs.

"Shit, I'm in a real mess here," Andy muttered, shaking like a leaf.

"Let's get undressed also Jack," George said.

"Sure thing man, sure fucking thing," Jack agreed.

Andy watched miserably as the two men stripped out of their clothes.

"Say Scrungy, is that a hard-on I see in your Fruit of The Looms bud?" George asked the construction worker.

"Funny, very fucking funny!" Andy responded sarcastically.

Then, naked, Jack and George knelt down at Andy's crotch. Andy's jaw dropped again as they rubbed their big hands over his briefs, sniffing them at the same time.

"Man, I would love to get a good whiff of these briefs of his after he's been out working in the sun all day," George laughed meanly and pressed his face to Andy's crotch.

"PERVERTS!!" Andy shouted.

In response to Andy's outburst the two men playfully snapped the elastic in the construction worker's briefs and squeezed his dick through the cotton material.

"Shall we at last taste Scrungy's dick?" George asked Jack, sounding oh so prim and proper.

"And why not at that?" Jack responded, sounding most hoity toity.

"Oh no... no..." Andy pleaded as George extracted his dick and balls out of the fly opening in his briefs. The studly construction worker's dick stood up straight and hard, dribbling pre cum as his balls dangled low.

"FUCK, what a piece!" George exclaimed. "What a goddamned succulent looking piece of meat! I go first!"

Slowly and ceremoniously George slurped and sucked Andy's dick into his mouth.

"NO, no!! Leave my dick alone man!! AWWWW God..."

But then, as he was being sucked on, Andy found himself in a forced sense of ecstasy.

"OOOOHHHH..." Andy groaned as Jack squatted behind him, pulled his briefs down and spread the construction worker's ass cheeks apart, revealing his bunghole.

"HEY, HEY, what the fuck are you doing back there?" Andy grunted. "OH NO, NO!!!"

As Andy hemmed and gasped Jack plunged his tongue into the construction worker's asshole and began licking it hungrily, sucking on the guy's ass walls as well. Andy stood helplessly and docilely still as the two men feasted on him and led him slowly to orgasm. George sucked Andy's dick roughly and savagely, using his teeth to scrape it, and nipping the very tip of it with his front-most teeth.

Behind him, Jack lapped like a hungry dog at Andy's hole, spitting in it, drenching it. Andy looked up at the ceiling and clenched his teeth, a feeling of disbelief coursing through him as the two men ran their hands over his hips, legs and feet.

"OOOHHHH GOD almighty, come on you two, give a guy a break huh?" Andy pleaded. "OOOOOO…"

As George and Jack worked on the construction worker they also toyed with his white sweat socks and black construction boots.

"UHHHHHNNN!!! Hey, easy with my dick, huh man?" Andy grunted, but then, suddenly, he felt it. "AWWW GAWD, I'm going to cum you fucking perverts! I'm going to shoot my goddamned load here!!! OH SHIT!!!!"

George quickly took Andy's dick out of his mouth and grabbed it tightly in hand. The construction worker squirted his manly juices all over his huge muscular chest. And as he came and came Jack slapped his ass hard.

"AAAARRRRRRNNN!!!!" Andy seethed in the forced ecstasy. "AAARRHHHH, my tits, my goddamned tits, GET THOSE CLAMPS OFF ME YOU GUYS!!!"

"Har, har, har for you Scrungy ol' boy, because you're finding out just how VERY sensitive a man's tits can become when he shoots his load, especially if said man's tits are locked in a pair of tight bighting tit clamps," George said, holding Andy's dick tighter and forcing the last of his splooge from him.

"AAAWWWW, you fucking twisted dudes," Andy cried loudly, looking down at his tits as they suffered and George holding his slowly shriveling dick.

When Andy was done splattering his mess and the pain in his clamped tits had subsided a bit George let go of his dick and the two men stood up. George draped an arm around Andy's broad shoulders.

"So your name is Andy huh bud?" George teased the guy.

"Y-yeah, now how about releasing me from these damned cuffs and getting the fuck out of my apartment!" Andy demanded. "You two had your fun with me..."

George smiled meanly, ran a finger through the cum on Andy's chest, and licked it off his finger.

"MMM... you taste real sweet Scrungy, but as for us leaving, you can forget that for now!" George said. "The fun is just starting! Jack let's get Scrungy roped to his bed and have us a good old fashioned butt fucking party!"

As he said it he playfully tugged on the tit clamps still on poor Andy's nipples.

"OWWWWW, N-no guys... *please don't... don't... fuck me...*" Andy begged.

"Looks to me like you need some sleep Scrungy," George said, grabbed a handful of Andy's salt and pepper hair and punched the construction worker hard across the face.

"PWAHHHHHH!!!!" Andy screamed and fell forward, over George's shoulders.

"Get the rope Jack," George said as he carried the now unconscious Andy Bowler further into the bedroom.

Sunday Night...

Andy woke up and found himself with an awful pain on the side of his face... and tied to his and his wife's bed. His wrists were roped tight to the bedposts, forcing him to remain on his knees. His Fruit of the Loom briefs were now off him along with his black construction boots. The construction worker was now left wearing just his white sweat socks. The tit clamps were still on his nipples, and his mouth was stuffed with one of George's socks, effectively gagging him.

"MMM..." Andy crooned as he came to, and then realized to his horror, the position he was tied in. "MMMMFFFFFF!!!!"

Taking in his situation and the heinous position he was tied in, the construction worker thrashed wildly on the bed, but try as he may, the ropes held him fast and would not give. He turned his head and saw his two, now naked, captors standing next to the bed and greasing up their mammoth sized erections with lubricant from their backpack.

"Who goes first George?" Jack asked breathlessly, as he greased up his huge cock.

"Seeing as my dick is bigger than yours, I do," George responded and his dick engorged even more when he saw the look of terror etched on Andy's handsome face.

George climbed onto the bed behind Andy and placed his hands on the construction worker's hips. He began inserting his huge dick inch by inch into the helpless construction worker.

"RRRMMMMFFFF!!!" Andy wailed miserably. "RHO, REASE, RHO..."

"Oh yeah Scrungy old scrounge, it sure feels nice back here," George panted as he entered the construction worker's back door.

Then, he meanly plunged his erection all the way in. Andy screamed behind his sock gag and saw stars as his vision blurred. George fucked him hard and mean, slapping the construction worker's hard buns at the same time.

"MMMMFFFFFFF..." Andy reeled, his tied hands clenched into huge construction worker sized fists.

"Oh fuck yeah Scrungy, you got some piece of ass back here," George grunted and spit onto Andy's ass cheeks, just for the fuck of it.

Jack reached underneath Andy and grabbed his dick. He jerked the tied construction worker off as George pumped his ass, not surprised to have found that Andy's own dick was hard as he was being fucked like some cheap whore.

As his dick was stroked Andy reeled and looked at Jack angrily, murder in his tear-filled eyes, thinking to himself, "How did this happen??? *How the fuck can this be happening???* Look at me, what a fucked up sight I am, tied up, gagged with a stinking sock in my mouth, and having my ass fucked, AND, being whacked the fuck off all at the same time."

Then, Andy's thoughts were cut short as he heard George announcing breathlessly, "Oh yeah, fuck yeah, I'm cumming, I'm fucking shooting my load Scrungy ol' boy!" George pounded Andy's ass hard as he spewed what seemed like his endless load, slapped the construction worker's buns firmly and filled and filled his hole with his juices. And then, seconds later, Andy himself shot his load as well, as Jack jacked him off.

"MMMMFFFF!!!" Andy blubbered behind the rancid sock that was in his mouth.

"Get up here Jack!" George panted as he let his shriveling dick slip out of Andy's hole. "It's your turn."

He climbed off the bed as Jack wasted no time, setting himself up behind the hapless construction worker.

"Okay Scrungy ol' boy, it's my turn now!" Jack said and Andy hung his head in frustration as Jack slowly entered his now cum sopped asshole.

"RRRFFFFFFF!!!" Andy screamed anew and his head popped up in a flash as Jack plunged his hard dick into his hole… and George reached under him to grab his dick. Andy looked over at George in utter disbelief.

"Going to shoot your juices for us again Scrungy," George cackled and stroked Andy's dick as Jack fucked him hard. "Come on big boy, I know you got it in you…"

"RRRRMMMMFFFF!!!" Andy ranted, spittle flying from the sides of his gagged sock stuffed mouth.

As he was fucked and stroked Andy squeezed his eyes shut in a mixture of forced ecstasy and pain.

And so it went for the next two hours, as the two men who had so easily captured him, took turns fucking the helpless construction worker's ass, over and over again, displaying an enormous amount of virility each, and jacking Andy off repeatedly, forcing load after load out of him. After two full hours the two men finally stopped. They untied Andy from the bedposts, the sock gag was taken out of the construction worker's craw and the tit clamps were removed from his nipples, getting a loud guttural scream of pain out of the poor guy, seeing as its well-known that when a pair of tit clamps come off a pair of nipples it hurts more than when they went on.

The construction worker lay there immobile on the bed, on his stomach, as the two men sat next to him, literally catching their breath.

"*Whoo, I need a break!*" George said happily.

"Me too man, me too," Jack agreed. "I'm beat!"

"*Whew,* if we're exhausted, imagine how Scrungy boy feels!" George laughed.

"Yeah, and wait'll he sees what's up next," Jack said and Andy lifted his head up off the bed, looking over at his captors in disbelief.

"OOOOhhh... pl-please guys... no more... *please...*" Andy begged to deaf ears.

"Jack, go to the kitchen and get a chair," George said.

"Sure thing buddy," Jack replied and dashed out of the bedroom.

Smiling evilly, George looked over at Andy. The muscular construction worker looked hot, sweated, and totally exhausted laying there on his stomach on the bed.

"Scrungy my boy, we have a special treat for you now!" George quipped.

"P-please... no... no..." Andy whimpered miserably.

The construction worker watched helplessly as George stood up. The fucking guy reached down, hoisted Andy up off the bed and slung him across his shoulders like a sack of dirty laundry, holding him tight by the wrists and ankles, insuring his immobility.

"UUUHHFFF, put me down you bastard!" Andy reeled, just as Jack returned to the bedroom with a wooden straight backed chair.

From his perch up on George's shoulders Andy watched as Jack put the chair down next to the bed and then from the backpack took a large, fat dildo. Andy's eyes opened wide in horror at the sight of the dildo.

"OH holy shit on a shingle again, no!!" Andy grunted and squirmed miserably on George's shoulders and in his tight grasp. "NO!!!"

"FUCK, help me with him Jack, this big boy is getting heavy!" George said and lowered Andy from his shoulders.

Holding the construction worker tight between them the two men lowered Andy's asshole onto the dildo, filling him slowly with it. They rocked him meanly up and down on it, working it methodically into his most private crevice. As Andy panted and grunted miserably it was seconds later when he was sitting with the large fat dildo in his asshole.

"ARRRGHHHHH, you fuckers!!!" Andy thundered and squirmed on the chair as George and Jack went to work tying him tightly to it.

Within moments Andy's hands were tied behind him, his upper body was roped tightly to the chair, accenting his chest and nipples really provocatively, his thighs were tied down to prevent him from getting up and getting the dildo out, and his feet were bound to the legs of the chair. Then, to Andy's terror, George tied a black silk blindfold over the construction worker's eyes… as a mean finishing touch.

"NO, *no, don't blindfold me too man… please…*" Andy begged as he felt George's fingers trailing through his hair a few times.

Then, the two men stepped in front of their bound up prize and looked him over lustfully.

"FUCK, just look at that hard-on of his," Jack said mockingly. "He can't deny he loves this shit!!"

"Hey, let's suck his balls, they look nice and yummy," George replied.

The two men squatted down in front of Andy and each of them took one of the construction worker's balls into their mouth. They sucked and lapped at Andy's testicles, HARD.

"AAAHHHRRRR!!!" Andy roared. "C'mon guys, leave my nuts alone huh???"

Feeling betrayed, Andy felt it as his dick stood up long and hard (despite having been pumped repeatedly) as George and Jack worked meanly on his balls.

"UUUHHHH!!!!" Andy sputtered, his head lolling back and forth as he suffered between pleasure and pain, pleasure from having his balls licked and sucked, and pain from the dildo tormenting his hole. Then, Andy felt a hand close around his throbbing erect dick.

"No, Aw naw!!!" Andy begged. *"C'mon you guys don't jack me the fuck off again!!"*

The burly construction worker slid up and down on the dildo as he was jerked off for the umpteenth time that evening. He shot his load in small squirts as the two men continued to torment his balls orally.

"OHHHHHHHH, fuckers, I'm cumming, AGAIN, I'm fucking cumming, OH GAWD!!" Andy swore and squirmed on the dildo as it tormented and fucked his hole.

The hand let go of Andy's dick and the construction worker then felt the two men finally stop sucking and working on his balls.

Later, Andy was untied from the chair, the dildo was out of his hole, and the blindfold had been taken off him.

He stood between the two men as Jack held his wrists tightly behind him and George held Andy by a handful of his salt and pepper colored hair.

"WH-what now?" Andy blithered miserably. "What the fuck now???"

"Now my friend, it's time to say good-night," George replied in Andy's handsome face. We'll be leaving! But we just want to say thank you for everything and for being so giving of yourself."

"HAR, HAR, HAR, very funny you bastard," Andy replied sarcastically as George raised a fist.

"Say good-night Scrungy," George laughed and Andy grimaced in impending terror.

"NO, no, don't clock me again man!!" Andy ranted, but nonetheless George delivered a hard and powerful blow to Andy's face. "YUFFFFFFF!!!"

Andy crumpled to the floor in a heap, totally unconscious.

"Let's get the fuck out of here," George said and he and Jack scurried from Andy's and Samantha's apartment.

A half hour later Andy came around. The exhausted and bruised construction worker dragged himself (naked except for his white sweat socks) to the bathroom. He stood and looked in the mirror.

"Oh damn it, those two bastards really worked me the fuck over," the construction worker said to himself as he took in the sight of the bruises on his face. "DAMN, DAMN, DAMN, and not to mention the fact that they raped the tar out of me, DAMN!!!"

In addition to the bruises Andy saw that his nipples were red, sore and still overly erect from having been clamped for so long, his dick was aching, his balls were swollen and throbbing and his asshole was burning from the long and repeated use the two rapists had made of it.

"Holy fuck, holy shit, if it's the last thing I do I WILL get even with those two perverts," Andy said to himself, shaking in his socks as he continued to look at his reflection in the mirror. "Muscle your way into a married man's home and use him like some cheap whore will they?? NO, they will pay… and pay dearly…"

Suddenly, a second wind propelled the hunky construction worker back to his bedroom. He looked out the window and an evil looking grin played across his face.

"That's their apartment directly across from here," Andy whispered to himself. "And all their lights are out. I bet working a stud like me over really exhausted them. WELL, they must be sound fucking asleep. Okay boys, now ol' Scrungy here has a big surprise for you two!!"

A short while later Andy was standing at the door to George and Jack's apartment. He was dressed in a fresh pair of blue cotton work pants, matching tee shirt, and his black scuffed up work boots.

"My turn guys," Andy said to himself, raised a fist to knock on the door, but suddenly the door opened in front of him. Before Andy could react a big hand grabbed his tee shirt and yanked him into the apartment.

"*ULLLPPP!!!*" Andy blubbered at the sudden twisted turn of events.

"I told you he'd be back for more Jack!" George laughed.

The door slammed shut and George's fist came crashing down on Andy's face.

In what seemed like seconds the construction worker found himself stripped to his work boots and white sweat socks. To his further dismay Andy found himself shackled in a spread-eagle position to a wall, gagged and blindfolded.

When his head cleared the two men were sucking his nuts...

About the Author

Christopher Trevor was born in July 1963 and grew up in New York City. As soon as he was old enough to know how he began writing fiction and has been writing gay erotic/fetish stories for the past ten to twelve years at this point. He became an avid reader as well from the time he knew how and reads everything from fiction, to non-fiction to biographies of interesting and unusual people, people who have made a difference or who have paved the way for others. Christopher attributes his writing artistic inspiration to artists such as Etienne, Tom of Finland, Tagame, The Hun, and most notably Joe T, who Christopher has had the pleasure of speaking with and even meeting over the last few years. Christopher states, "Joe T encouraged me to write about my fetish because I was embarrassed about it at the time. Joe T said that when we are embarrassed about something that makes it even more enticing somehow." Christopher totally agreed and never stopped writing in this genre. Erotic writers who inspired Christopher Trevor were: Tom Shaw (author of "That Day at the Quarry), C.S. White (author of Big Sur), Larry Townsend (author of countless erotic novels), and Mason Powell (author of the classic story "The Brig.")

Christopher discovered that not only did he enjoy writing erotic tales but that after his first bondage experience he had a genuine flair for it. Writing to erotic oriented magazines about his first bondage experience truly opened the floodgates for Christopher where this style of writing is concerned. Christopher thanks the handsome and muscular "Greg" for that experience way back in time. Christopher took "Creative Writing" courses every semester during his high school years and while other friends of his stopped writing what they loved to write about as time went on Christopher never let a day go by when he didn't write something… "I feel that if I don't write every day I will die," Christopher has said many times over.

Foot fetish stories and all things related; spanking fetish, erotic shaving, muscle bondage, tickle torture, and hardcore stories are just a few of the areas of gay eroticism that Christopher enjoys writing about and inspiring in others as well. As one internet buddy said to Christopher where the black socks fetish is concerned, "Until I started talking with you I never gave a thought to my socks when I got dressed for work in the morning. Now when I pull my dress socks on every morning I get a chill up my spine."

Christopher is proud of the erotic effect he has on people…

Christopher Trevor is also the author of:

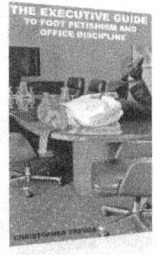

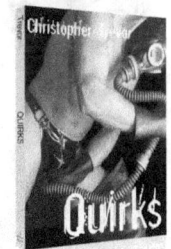

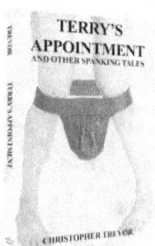

 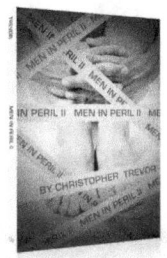 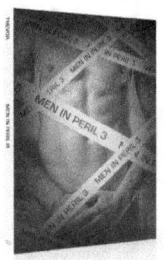